BALKAN BOMBSHELLS

CONTEMPORARY
WOMEN'S
WRITING
FROM
SERBIA
AND
MONTENEGRO

Compiled and translated by
WILL FIRTH

istrosbooks

First published in 2023
by Istros Books
London, United Kingdom
www.istrosbooks.com

© Istros Books, 2023
Translation © Will Frith

Cover design: frontispis.hr
Typesetting: pikavejica.com

ISBN: 978-1-912545-84-1

The publishers would like
to express their thanks to
the Arts Council England
for the financial support
that made the publication
of this book possible.

Supported using public funding by

**ARTS COUNCIL
ENGLAND**

The EU is not responsible for the
views expressed in this publication or
in conjunction with the activities for
which the mobility support was used.

This project was made possible
by a European Union travel grant
from the i-Portunus consortium
headed by the Goethe Institut,
with Institut français and Izolyatsia.

CONTENTS

INTRODUCTION

This collection of writing by strong female authors is the fruit of happenstance. It began with a windfall travel scholarship and one-month stay in Belgrade in late 2021. The idea of compiling a collection of women's stories came from my host organisation, the KROKODIL Centre for Contemporary Literature. It, and the team of the Biber contest for socially engaged short stories, helped me select a stock of powerful texts by young women writers from Serbia. But the material was insufficient for a satisfying-sized book, and since I have many acquaintances in neighbouring countries, particularly Montenegro, I decided to extend the scope. The result is this multi-generational, Serbian-Montenegrin prose anthology. I approached Istros Books in London, and the publisher was immediately taken by the idea. This is our twelfth book together.

Women's writing in the region of southeastern Europe and the Balkans, specifically in the countries that were once part of Yugoslavia, is definitely not a new phenomenon. Isolated female writers have made their mark since the Middle Ages, such as the Orthodox nun Jefimija (1349–1405), the poet Anica Bošković from Dubrovnik (1714–1804) and the Croatian children's writer Ivana Brlić-Mažuranić (1874–1938). With the spread of compulsory education in the twentieth century and the socio-political aspirations of both upper-class women and the socialist movement, the number of female writers grew. Yet even today it is often a struggle for women to assert themselves and 'come out' as writers in a patriarchal society where writing is widely perceived as a male domain.

Three late 20th-century writers relatively well known outside the Balkans are Slavenka Drakulić (*How We Survived Communism and Even Laughed*, and many other books), Daša Drndić (*Trieste, Belladonna*) and Dubravka Ugrešić (*The Museum of Unconditional Surrender*, etc.). Few female writers from Serbia or Montenegro have enjoyed an international breakthrough as yet, but mention should be made of Vesna Goldsworthy, who writes predominantly in English (*Inventing Ruritania, Monsieur Ka*, etc.), the poet Ana Ristović, Marija Knežević (*Ekaterini*, Istros Books) and Jelena Lengold (*Fairground Magician*, Istros Books), who is represented in this collection.

It is probably fair to say that no female writers from the region of former Yugoslavia can make a living from creative writing alone – readerships are small and the creative sector is underfunded. The same applies for the vast majority of their male colleagues. Writers are aware of their position and can arguably allow themselves greater freedom than if they were pandering to the purported expectations of 'the market'; on the other hand, there are often other pressures, for example to conform to national norms and canons.

This collection brings together a great variety of styles and themes. Most of the pieces are short stories, but three are stand-alone excerpts from novels, and one is a set of intense diary entries (Marijana Dolić's 'Notes from the attic').

Many of the stories deal with amorous relationships, and several look into traditional female roles (particularly

Bojana Babić's 'A man worth waiting for') and motherhood (Ana Miloš's 'Peace'). Babić's piece and two others have a decidedly meta twist, and a few others have a surreal or magical side (especially Marijana Čanak's feminist revenge story, 'Awakened'). Unavoidably, some of the stories deal with the wars in ex-Yugoslavia (Milica Rašić's poignant 'Smell'), the fall of Milošević (Svetlana Slapšak's 'I'm writing to you from Belgrade') and experience of exile or living abroad (Olja Knežević's 'Trapped'). Fear of male violence is reflected in Zvonka Gazivoda's 'Something, at least' and Katarina Mitrović's 'Small death'. The process of writing is an issue in Svetlana Kalezić-Radonjić's 'The title' and Andrea Popov-Miletić's 'Young Pioneers, we are seaweed'. Several of the pieces are highly entertaining, such as Jelena Lengold's well-crafted 'Do you remember me?' and Dana Todorović's exquisitely ironic 'Redundancy'. Similar vividness is found in 'Everything' by Jovanka Vukanović and 'The day with the head' by Slađana Kavarić-Mandić. The sixteen sketches in Tijana Živaljević's 'Home libraries' bring together people's often quirky and inconsistent relationship to books – treasures, heirlooms, ballast when moving house, or hotly contested possessions when a couple splits up.

Montenegro seceded from the last manifestation of rump Yugoslavia ('Serbia and Montenegro') in 2006 after a narrowly won referendum. But there are undeniable historical links between the two countries. Six of the seventeen authors are from Montenegro. Lena Ruth Stefanović's 'Zhenya' clearly expresses a Montenegrin identity, whereas this is less perceptible with the other five. All the stories in the collection were written in the polycentric language formerly known as Serbo-Croat(ian), today often referred to with the acronym BCMS, i.e. Bosnian/Croatian/Montenegrin/Serbian. All of the authors wrote in the Latin script, although the Cyrillic alphabet has equal official status in both Serbia and Montenegro; this is reflective of a long-term shift in preferences. None of the writers from Montenegro used the new letters ś and ź introduced there in the noughties to represent the phonemes of local dialects – even proponents of Montenegrin independence sometimes feel them to be an imposition.

It should be emphasised that there was no *a priori* reason for bringing nominally Serbian and nominally Montenegrin authors together in this collection. It was a purely pragmatic decision based on personal contacts and familiarity with the literary scene. Ethnic-national definitions are shallow, if not misleading. As Stefanović asks rhetorically in her story, '[can] literature be compartmentalised in terms of cultural heritage, or is good writing inevitably secular and universal?'

We are proud to be presenting these bold, compelling female voices, several of which are being published in English for the first time.

Dobra književnost ne poznaje granice! Good literature knows no borders!

WILL FIRTH

NOTE ON THE PRONUNCIATION OF NAMES

We have maintained the original spelling of proper nouns. Vowels are pronounced roughly as in Italian. The consonants are pronounced as follows:

c = ts, as in *bits*
č = ch
ć = similar to č, like the t in *future*
dž = g, as in *general*
đ = similar to dž
j = y, as in *yellow*
r = trilled as in Scottish; sometimes used as a vowel, e.g. 'Srđan,' roughly *Sirjan*
š = sh
ž = like the s in *pleasure*

Bojana Babić

A MAN WORTH WAITING FOR

Everything that Marijana owned could be fitted in the old blue bag that Vesna brought from Macedonia when Budimir went to find himself a wife strong enough to chop wood and milk four cows twice daily. Vesna was completely to his liking; the only thing that bothered him was that she stood with a cigarette while cooking at the stove and thought no one could see her, and Budimir had always had eyes in the back of his head, on his ears and everywhere else. He promised Marijana's brother Miodrag that he'd buy him a bicycle if he told him every day what Vesna did while he wasn't at home. Marijana once found Miodrag in the yard, leaning in through the window of their unfinished kitchen. 'What are you gawping at?' she whispered, and he put his hand over her mouth and thrust her to the ground. Miodrag heard the roar of the tractor and rushed out the gate. 'Mum's smoking!' he shouted, but Budimir didn't see him and didn't hear him over the noise of the engine, so, as usual, he swung his leg to jump down from the tractor and knocked out two of Miodrag's teeth. Miodrag got a new bike out of it, but not any new teeth.

Marijana wasn't interested in bikes; she always preferred home-made bread, lard and chicken liver, but most of all the plum preserves she scoffed before bed while watching turbo-folk programmes on TV and imagining she was one of the singers in a tight skirt and tiger bra. Marijana knew the words to every song that echoed loudly from her room, a room with unpainted walls in the old house where they all lived together. Budimir had built a new house next to it, but no one was allowed to go there, not even Miodrag, for whom the house was intended. 'When you bring a girl and have children, the house will be yours,' Budimir said.

'When are you going to marry off Marijana?' the neighbours would ask, and Budimir would twiddle his fingers and say: 'When the right man comes along.' Mr Right. That was the man who'd come to Budimir and tell him he'd like to take Marijana home and never bring her back: a slim, hard-working young fellow with house, land and cattle. Marijana always imagined she'd meet Mr Right down at the canal. She'd sit on the grass with the other eligible girls and watch the boys splash around in the shallow water and swim to the other bank. They'd come back ruddy and smiling, emboldened by their feat, and approach Marijana and her girlfriends. Mr Right would sit down on her towel without asking, offer her a wet hand and introduce himself. He'd ask which village she was from and why he hadn't seen her at the canal before. Marijana would poke her finger in the soft earth and conceal a smile. She hadn't come because she couldn't swim. Mr Right would stand up and take Marijana by the hand. 'Don't, please!' she'd cry, but Mr Right wouldn't listen. He'd lead her into the shallows and first give her a good splashing, then he'd pull her deeper into the water, to her friends' cheers. 'Don't you trust me?' Mr Right would ask with a sly smile because he knew Marijana had never been taught to say 'no' at home. Now up to their waist in the water, he'd motion for her to turn onto her belly and let herself down into the water, above his muscular arms. Marijana would be afraid but obey him. She'd look towards the bank and see that her friends were gone – no one was there but her and Mr Right. She'd clench her teeth and swim, and Mr Right would take his arms away. 'See, it's not so scary,' he'd say as she doggy-paddled with her eyes closed. Mr Right then grabbed her by the waist and slowly slipped his hand under her swimming costume.

In reality, Marijana had never even been to the canal, and now it was winter anyway, the river had frozen over, and Marijana was actually getting married. She packed heavy, thick jumpers and dresses that belonged to Vera, but that she'd never seen her wear, and she put on a long white one that was tight around the waist. Her friend Biljana came to do her eyes, cheeks and lips.

The man in question had chosen the biggest piglet on the farm, paid a good price for it and then sat down in the yard to taste Budimir's *rakija*. 'Nenad,' he said, shaking Marijana's hand and smiling to reveal a few bad teeth. Marijana didn't dare to speak while Nenad talked about his house in the forest, far from the village and the neighbours.

'It's peaceful and quiet where I am,' he said and looked at Marijana. 'Do you also like peace and quiet?'

Marijana shrugged her shoulders. Budimir sent her to cut some bacon and she obediently set off for the kitchen, feeling Nenad's gaze on her buttocks.

'You know, Marijana, that forester is a good man,' Vesna tossed to her in passing. When she went out into the yard with the tray, Budimir was gone.

'Sit with me,' Nenad said and lit a cigarette, making sure the smoke didn't get in Marijana's face. 'How old are you?' he asked.

'Twenty-four,' Marijana answered softly.

'I was sixteen when you were born – this big. I had no beard, and no sense either. And today, nothing's changed,' Nenad started to laugh, so Marijana laughed too. 'You have a nice smile,' he said and tucked a strand of greasy hair behind her ear.

Marijana was relieved when Budimir returned with a squealing piglet in his arms. They put it in a sack, and then in the boot of Nenad's red Zastava 101. 'She'll make a good sow,' Nenad declared and drove back into the forest.

'Marijana, the forester wants to marry you. That's why he came.' Budimir stated. 'He's alone there in the house. He needs a woman who knows how to work, to help.'

'To be there when he needs her,' Vesna added.

Marijana looked at her hands. Her fingers were thick, and she'd chewed her nails so much as a child that they no longer grew enough to cover the flesh. She wanted to chew them even more, until they were gone.

'It's your decision. Let me know tomorrow,' Budimir said and left.

Marijana would lay her head on the pillow every night and immediately fall asleep, but now she was tossing and turning in bed.

Her friend Bilja let the phone ring for a long time before answering. Her soft, sleepy voice finally answered, 'I knew it was you.'

Marijana twisted the phone cord nervously, 'A forester has asked me to marry him.' Bilja laughed. 'And? What did you tell him?'

'Nothing,' Marijana admitted.

'Is he handsome?' Bilja asked.

'I don't know – he's not ugly,' Marijana admitted. 'It's just he's older than us. His face is serious.'

'It's good when a man is serious,' Bilja replied.

'How does it feel when you get married?' Marijana asked and Bilja sighed.

'It's good, only my husband drinks a lot. But he doesn't bother me. It's not a problem. He drinks and then sleeps.'

Marijana and Nenad got married in the church behind which she'd had her first kiss with a boy from Vršac who'd come to watch a match; he took her round into the dark, stuck his tongue down her throat and slid his hands under her T-shirt. He fondled her until Miodrag appeared, broke his collarbone and called Marijana a slut. Marijana got a fright when she stepped out in front of all the guests with their expectations, but the way Nenad was looking she could see nothing in his eyes, and that calmed her. Vesna and Budimir were beaming proudly, while Miodrag stared at the floor. When the priest asked, Marijana said 'yes', Nenad said 'yes' and kissed her, and everyone started clapping as if it all surprised them.

Afterwards, Marijana sat in the same place as when Nenad asked if she liked peace and quiet, only now there was no peace or quiet, but loud music and lots of people. Vesna was serving pork and bread, Budimir brought out aged *rakija* he'd saved for 'when our child gets married', except he'd thought that child would be their son. Nenad poured Marijana one glass and then another, while Bilja pulled her arm: 'You have to dance so you'll have a happy life.' Marijana's eyes were falling shut and she wanted to lie down for a bit, to rest her feet from the tight high-heeled shoes she couldn't walk in, but where could she go? Vesna, Dušica, Miroslava, Ljubica and Aunt Rada were in the house with other neighbours and reminiscing about their own weddings. Marijana just wanted to be alone for a little while, so she furtively took the key to the new house, went through the dank hall, took her shoes off and lay down carefully on the new bed, which was covered with musty linen.

'You shouldn't have drunk,' Miodrag said, pushing Marijana's legs so he could sit down next to her. Marijana raised her head and rubbed her red ear, which hurt as if someone had tried to tear it off her head. Her fingers felt thick lines running from her lips to her forehead caused by the coarse linen. 'How long have I slept?' Marijana asked. Miodrag burst into tears before he could answer. Confused, Marijana stroked his prematurely bald head, which reminded her of an eggshell, but Miodrag pushed her away, wiped his eyes and snotty nose on his sleeve and went. Marijana sighed deeply, then slowly pulled the shoes onto her swollen feet and followed her brother. The yard was still full. The women were leaning out of the kitchen window and smiling, and the men were toasting. Nenad took Marijana by the waist. 'I'll look after you,' he said and planted her on the front seat of his Zastava. Vesna wanted to cry, but Budimir stopped her: 'She's not going to the end of the world, only to the end of the forest.'

Nenad and Marijana left the village, turned towards the hills and passed a weekend settlement that had once been popular with Belgraders but was now overgrown with robinia. They entered a scraggly pine forest, and Nenad didn't look ahead while driving, but at Marijana. He put his hand on her knee and said he'd prepared everything for her. Nothing could be seen anymore except a plot of land in the car's headlights, and Marijana was afraid they'd veer off the road and hit a tree or run into a deer, but Nenad had been living in the forest for a long time and knew it like the pocket of the coat he now wore over his wedding suit. They entered the yard, where they were greeted by a small dog without a tail. Nenad took Marijana's blue bag, and then he lifted her up and carried her into the bedroom. 'Don't be afraid, you'll be fine,' he said. Then he coughed and needed a while to settle down. 'Where's the bathroom?' Marijana asked and he pointed with a gnarled finger. Marijana aimed for the hole in the floor, but the hot liquid ran down her shoes. She went back to the bedroom, where Nenad was lying with his arms outstretched. Marijana turned off the light and went up to the bed. Nenad took off her dress and laid his head on her sagging breasts. 'We'll do it tomorrow,' he yawned and turned over onto his belly. Marijana put on the nightgown that Vesna packed for her first wedding night, white with pink dots. She crawled carefully under the blanket Nenad was lying on, then curled up beside him and watched his shoulders rise and fall in a steady rhythm until he drifted off to sleep.

Parts of the guests' faces mingled and merged with one another: Budimir's eyes with Nenad's, Dušica's mouth with that of her daughter and Uncle Marko's gaunt cheeks with Vesna's; Miodrag's pug nose fused with Suzi's long crooked nose and the noses of the other neighbours and everyone who was revelling at the wedding, until they became one countenance that Marijana recognised – the man worth waiting for. She felt a dull pain in her crotch, and when she opened her eyes Nenad was above her, groaning and squeezing her. He smelled like a man who's lived a long time. Marijana kissed him, and then she felt something warm caress her legs. 'A son,' Nenad declared and gave her a peck on the cheek.

Marijana Čanak

AWAKENED

She was born still encased in the placenta. The women had
fussed around her mother's belly for two days, massaging,
praying and chanting. When everything calmed down, she
slipped out all by herself. It was a quarter to three. She
wriggled up to her mother's breast herself and started suck-
ling. The feeding was more painful than giving birth. The
baby bit and pulled as if extracting underground milk from
the swollen nipples. When she was full and clean, she cried
loudest. The women came running to help again, and they
took turns cuddling and rocking her. She wore out each one
of them. The first came down with welts on her face, the
next started to go grey, and the third developed a bunion.
Her mother already had three children, but she was crazed
as if this was her first. She pulled out her hair, tore at her
breasts and frantically scratched her thighs.

'What did I do wrong to get you?' she leaned over the
cot and screamed. She mourned for her old life until her
husband grabbed her by the neck and squeezed her against
the wall like a fly.

'Who did you make her with? Tell me!' he glared at
her with bloodshot eyes and shouted. 'You know full well
I never fail! My seed is good. It makes male children, not
monsters. Whore breeds whore!'

He let her slide down the wall to slump like a battered bag. He spat in the cot on the way out and rushed to the nearest tavern to drown his disgust; not returning for days. To prevent their daughter from demolishing the house, they took her away to her grandmother to mind. There she learned to walk and speak. Later they brought her back.

'She'll have work to do around the house. She can wait on her brothers. Let her learn.'

When she was five, her mother taught her to make bread. She taught her patiently.

'Now we'll cover the dough and let it rise.'

As soon as her mother turned away to do some other chore, the girl tore off pieces of dough and made them into little figures. She lined them up in front of her, stabbed them with a fork and groaned as if she were they; she chopped off one's head and made the others play with it like a ball; she tore the limbs off the disobedient, transplanted them onto the backs of others and laughed at the company of little monsters that multiplied beneath her hands. Her mother was horrified and stared at her agape.

'I'll throttle her! May the bread forgive me,' she hissed and lunged at the girl, but an intent gaze stopped her.

'Shh!' she put her finger to her mouth. 'Can you hear? Someone's wailing!'

Her mother listened as if spellbound, and her heart pounded in her ears. She heard crying and calling for help, widow's weeds rustling and being drenched with tears. An open grave yawned, candles fizzled and wreaths were plaited.

'Someone's going to die!' the girl said, and her mother was taken aback. She clouted her on the mouth, then picked up the scattered little figures and pressed them back into the dough. *It's childish nonsense,* she tried to calm herself. *She*

turns everything upside down and invents things in her games.
We all did when we were little, and later we forgot it all.

The next day she kneaded the bread herself. *Let her be, she's still small. There's time for her to learn,* she thought and stoked the fire. No sooner than she'd put the bread in the oven, her husband entered and crashed onto the couch.

'My old lady died,' he said and covered his eyes.

When she turned seven, they reluctantly sent her to school.

'School is for shirkers. They cram kids' heads with all sorts of stuff and turn them into sluggards!' her father grumbled.

Her mother glowered and tugged as she plaited the girl's hair.

'Let her go then. She's no good for anything else!' he concluded and spat in the doorway. 'Why do you comb her all day? It's not as if she's getting married!' he yelled and brandished his fist. She raised her hands to protect her head, while the girl dashed out of the house, running as fast as her legs would carry her, without looking back.

She loved books at school but couldn't stand other children. She kept double exercise books – one for herself, and the other with imaginary lessons and fake assignments in case someone asked if they could copy from her. Soon no one asked her for anything and they left her alone. She didn't spend the breaks with anyone or share her snacks. The teachers didn't dispute she was bright, but her cleverness was uncanny and sent a chill down their spines.

'As bright as a button,' they whispered. 'But even if she's the brightest in the world, she won't be happy!'

In the fourth year, she was accused of stealing a watch. Everyone in the class stared at her when the golden-haired girl from the first row stood in front of the teacher and explained in a weepy voice:

'My blue watch. It does up like a bracelet. My uncle bought it for me in Vienna. My mum will kill me if I don't find it! I just want it back. I won't tell anyone! Please don't punish anyone ... just let me have back what's mine!'

She felt all those looks – they got under her skirt and crawled over her irritated skin like ants, searching every inch of her body for the blue watch.

'She swallowed it!' they whispered, pointed at her and laughed maliciously,but she carried on drawing in one of her double exercise books without the slightest hint of anxiety and didn't take her eyes off the paper. The teacher demanded that everyone empty their bags and pockets, so all the students obediently heaped textbooks, exercise books, pencil cases and leftover sandwiches on their desks. Meanwhile, she finished the drawing, enlivened it with some quick shading and closed the exercise book. She was content. She leaned down to put the exercise book back in her bag, but the teacher's hand intercepted it. He tightened his grip around her wrist and the exercise book fell to his feet.

'Let me see what kind of records you're keeping here,' he mocked and stared at the drawing. His lips trembled, his face changed colour and she felt his pulse on her wrist.

'What's this?' he shouted and turned the drawing towards the class.

'A watch, a watch!' resounded like an echo in the classroom.

'My watch!' the golden-haired girl jumped and reached out her hand as if to tear it out of the exercise book.

The teacher rubbed his temples and hushed the class; he could have sworn he saw the hands move in the drawing. When everyone was quiet, the watch could be heard ticking, and the class broke into an uproar. The teacher dropped the exercise book as if it were cursed.

'Give back the watch!' he commanded.

'I haven't got it. That's just a drawing,' she said calmly. The teacher slapped her.

'Where's the watch?' he yelled.

'I know where it is, but I'd rather not say,' she replied soberly, looking him straight in the eyes. He slapped her once more, and her lip began to bleed.

'Speak up!'

She wiped the blood with her handkerchief and adjusted her plait.

'It's on your wrist,' she said. The teacher swung his arm to strike her once more, but it remained in mid-air, as if petrified. A blue children's watch was engraved on his skin. And with every tick the clasp sank deeper into his flesh. They couldn't get it off without cutting into his skin.

She attended the rest of primary school three hundred kilo-metres away, sent to a great-aunt who was alleged to be the mother of many, although she'd never given birth. Her great-aunt lived alone in a small house. She gave her a bed in the hallway, and next to the headboard was a cardboard box full of newly hatched chickens.

'So that you take care of them for me!' she said with satisfaction, in a tone that promised that everything in life would fall into place one day.

Her great-aunt didn't pester her, the chickens pooed on her bed like giant double-headed birds, and she took revenge on them in her dreams: she dreamed of plucking them alive, tearing off their legs and throwing them away over the roofs, then she'd paint their beaks and made them into a colourful necklace.

Marijana Čanak

The new school was good. Her great-aunt didn't stop her from doing her homework, and she taught her practical skills. She trimmed her fringe, and she bought her a short, chequered skirt and a white blouse.

'When you see a boy you like, do this,' she said, and pulled the fringe over her eyes. '*When it sticks in my eyes, may every cockle of his heart warm to me!* You say that three times and then puff between your boobs. Any one of them will be yours!'

She wasn't interested in boys, so she just puffed the fringe off her forehead, but she remembered every one of her great-aunt's words.

In biology classes, she discovered a new world under the microscope: onion skin, birch leaf, moss, chamomile petal, dragonfly wing, fly eye, moth antennae, the golden dust of a swallowtail, a peppercorn, saliva and a human hair. Snippets of the world containing whole new worlds. She was ecstatic – she wanted to put everything onto the glass slide and then under the microscope. She could spend her life doing nothing else.

She'd ask her great-aunt to buy her a microscope, but first she had to explain in detail what that was so she didn't end up with glasses on her nose. Her great-aunt bought her a desk lamp with a magnifying glass. She wasn't thrilled, but the class where the biology teacher dissected a frog soon gave the device a purpose. A small anatomy class took place at her desk, and pride and excitement stirred in her chest. The teacher stretched out the frog and skilfully cut the skin to reveal its inner organs. The frog was alive and pulsating. The teacher gave her metal tweezers to touch its bare femur. She'd gladly have pulled it out and kept it as a souvenir. The other girls watched with concealed horror, fearing the frog could jump when touched and cling to someone's face. The frog still pulsated silently, consigning its dissected body to science in the children's hands. She tapped the frog's bone and imagined with glowing eyes: *What if we squished its heart in under the microscope, immersed its lungs in water, unwound its intestines…* But the class soon ended and the frog was crumpled into a plastic cup.

'Who's going to throw it in the toilet?' the teacher glanced around the class while holding the pulsating cup.

Everyone backed away, but her hand shot up. She gripped the cup in her hand and strode down the corridor, determined to repeat the experiment at home. She dissected frogs, lizards and small rodents under the magnifying glass. It excited her how alive they were as they died.

She reluctantly spent the holidays at home, lonely as in a foreign land. She helped her mother and was bored by the work: scrubbing the floors, peeling potatoes, tenderising the meat, polishing the plates and hanging up the laundry. Her mother never stopped.

'The two of us can finish in an hour. For two pairs of hands it's nothing!' she said. When she enumerated all the tasks, she always began with *I didn't ask you.* 'I didn't ask you, but would you gather up those apples? Could you sift the flour and spread out the sheet of pastry? Bake the pie? Take it to your brothers?'

She'd always been alienated from her brothers. They didn't like her hanging around and were suspicious of her food. They looked askance at how round she'd become, they avoided her eyes, and they didn't know what to talk about with her. The eldest collected badges. When their mother sent her to clean up after him, she took the opportunity to look at his collection. She peered at the backing they were pinned to – something like that would come in handy for her golden-winged beetles and butterflies. She'd also pin locusts, especially the huge yellow ones with red legs; they just needed to be cleaned of their insides so they wouldn't rot. Once her brother caught her reading his badges with her fingers and frowned like a father in miniature.

'Hey, what are you doing?'

'Just looking.'

'Only the blind look with their fingers.'

Her middle brother loved hunting and was learning to stuff animals. She might have a common topic of interest with him, but she felt he'd make fun of every question she asked. The head of a dead deer protruded from the wall of his room. Its horns were slightly larger than a goat's, its eyes were like glass and its muzzle was dry and black. Sometimes the way the light fell into the room made the deer look as if it were smiling, as if triumphing after having broken through the wall. She'd pat it, whisper secrets in its hairy ear, wrap her arms around its severed neck, and cool her head next to its.

The youngest brother hid books under his bed. Lots of books. If she took one to amuse herself, no one would notice. She took the thickest and marvelled at how light it was. When she opened it, she saw the pages were cut away in the middle and that it served as a box, where her brother kept smutty pictures. Images of sprawling bodies, naked skin, spread legs, protruding buttocks and huge teeth around a purple nipple. She shuddered as she looked at them, but at the same time something made her browse further and devour all those bodies with her eyes. She put the book back in its place and borrowed it occasionally ... until her youngest brother told her out of the blue:

'Go home! Why did you come here? You just stir things up!'

She returned to her great-aunt's in the autumn and never went home again. In the final year of primary school, in biology, she already knew the whole year's material and excelled. Her knowledge of bones and muscles, the network of blood vessels, neural maps and lymph nodes – how everything that pulsates beneath the skin fitted together – was awe-inspiring.

'It would be a shame not to enrol in the lyceum. Such talent shouldn't be wasted!' the teacher told her.

The girl levitated on the way back from school, the ground beneath her feet was fluffy and everything seemed to fall apart like a dandelion head. She couldn't wait to ask her great-aunt what a lyceum was. Her great-aunt was less than enthusiastic.

'It's that building near the market. I've heard they torture children there.'

She'd gladly agree to be tortured just so as not to be sent home.

'It's best you learn a trade,' her great-aunt tried to persuade her. 'Here, I'll teach you to sew. My eyes aren't what they used to be, but I still know the basics. Whoever's measurements you take is a bird in your hand. Even if you take in his suit here and let it out there, he'll be indebted to you forever. What more do you need for a good life? I'll teach you everything!'

She looked at her great-aunt as if about to cry. If forced to sew, she'd swallow all the buttons and stab herself all over with poisoned needles; she'd fall asleep out of spite and only wake up when everyone she knew was dead.

'Alright, but what good will the lyceum be?'

'I'll have biology three times a week. And four years to think.'

Her great-aunt grumbled. She was suspicious of going down that path, and she didn't know anyone who was happy in science, let alone education. They were in that treadmill all their life – when would they do some living?

But in the end she gave in, 'Have it your way.'

She felt she was meeting like-minded people at the lyceum but soon realised she was wrong. Her name disturbed the famous and respectable surnames in the roll book, and she was proud of it from the first day until the last. She despised the boys with guitars instead of backbones and called them invertebrates who stole others' chords. She rolled her eyes when the girls talked about make-up and waterproof eye-lashes, or about needing to abstain from chocolate if you wanted your face to be as smooth as paper. She was sick of couples groping around in corners, scratching initials in hearts and cracking their knuckles in class as if it were longer than a Siberian winter. The ugly, dowdy, spotty and maladjusted girls wanted her to tribe up with them, but that offended her. She preferred not to have anyone. She didn't go to birthday parties, didn't go out on Friday nights, and boycotted organised skiving and excursions where sex games alternated with visits to monasteries. None of that bothered her as much as the fact that biology wasn't what it used to be. If a horned cow and a hornless bull cross, what is the probability of the calf having horns? She wasn't interested in the slightest. By the end of school, her thirst for discovery had been quenched.

In Physical Education, she didn't sweat from the running and stretching, but from uneasiness. The teacher had a malevolent look. He ordered them around with a whistle between his teeth, and she felt like a circus poodle. He lined up the girls and stared at their chests, judging whether they were lush, white and firm enough. Something in his eye reminded her of her angry father, her suspicious brothers and the unfair teacher. Everything she'd tried to avoid converged in that man. Long after the class had ended she could still feel his eyes on her skin, so she rubbed herself with a rough towel, scouring until it was red. She'd flay herself just to erase him. In a gymnastics class, he held his arm around her waist for too long as he was positioning her on the beam.

'You would've fallen if I'd let go!' he shouted, making fun of how clumsy and unstable she was. 'Keep your balance!' He straightened her back and slipped his fingers under the clasp of her bra. Her face flushed like the sound of a whistle.

She came to the next PE class without her sports gear and asked to be excused.

'Why would I excuse you?' the teacher taunted.

'My period.'

'Louder, I can't hear you.'

'I've got my period,' she repeated. The teacher flipped through his notebook, found her name, and pressed it with his index finger as if crushing a stray insect.

'Do you have it twice a month? You know I have a right to check? After class, in my office. Or it's into the gym now!'

She didn't move from the bench.

'Good,' he said, circled her name in red and blew his whistle.

She ran back to her great-aunt's as if a pack of devils were at her heels. She sat in the shower and let the water wash away everything, and the shame, and the blood inside. She heard her great-aunt dozing in the armchair, went up to her, crouched down, hugged her knees and spread her wet hair over her lap.

'Teach me to sew.'

'Really?' her great-aunt started and absently caressed the girl's face. 'You're back early. Dry your hair or you'll catch a cold.'

'I will. And then will you teach me?'

'Uh-huh. What shall it be?'

'A dress for the school dance.'

'We'll have lunch first. When we're hungry we're nervous, and the needle doesn't obey nervous fingers.'

Her great-aunt climbed up on a chair, opened the closet, took out a roll of turquoise silk and stroked it like a sleeping child.

'I knew this day would come,' she chirruped.

She taught the girl after lunch. She marked the fabric with chalk, cut the pieces and pinned them together, wound the bobbin and threaded the sewing machine, which purred away like a contented cat. The girl gathered up the snippets and made them into a stuffed doll. Her great-aunt laughed.

'What's that for? You're too big to play babies!'

'For practice.'

The doll was male, had a slit for a mouth, a whistle in it, and pointed buttons for eyes. *If the fringe sticks in, needles will stick in even better*, she thought and pierced the doll's groin. As the needle stabbed the doll, she watched with her third eye. She saw spat-out balls of hair in the gym, the floor stained with urine, a crushed whistle and two wrenched-out teeth. She saw him toothless and bald, wetting his own bed, yet grateful to God he wasn't pissing blood. She saw a celebration where no one asked why he wasn't there.

Satisfied with this vision, she buried the doll. Then she slipped her fingers in between her legs and marked her forehead with a red dot. She was awakened.

Marijana Dolić

NOTES FROM THE ATTIC
(excerpt)

10. 11 Faith

Thoughts and words have vanished. I've been gone for a long time, as have you. Parting with the word 'goodbye' is a mere formality of a separation that happened long before. We influenced the matrix; we took a side. Mine is that of light. Light is most effective in the dark. I'm sorry I'm not the right match for you, I'm sorry you've been wasting your time and energy on destruction. I've found a way and am leaving.

I think of all the wonderful people who've left a mark of light on my heart: thank you for existing. I believe this is the best possible existence, according to what I've read and heard ... though it's all irrelevant if you don't preserve your sanity. No matter how much we resist, the curse of our ancestors' genes catches up with us in moments of carelessness. Just one instant is enough for all our work and commitment to go up in smoke as if it never existed. Strange. Everything pales and disappears. What remains is family. Perhaps. What if you don't have anyone? What if you have nothing?

Can you escape from the primitivism that dogs and haunts you? Everything that makes you happy seems to disappear, to vanish. If you view life through rose-coloured glasses, which is much less painful, everything occurs for our highest good. You need to believe, believe ... 'What does that even mean?' you ask yourself. What is faith? Confused, you rummage through dusty folders in your mind, looking for the letter F. 'Ah, here it is. F for faith. F, F, F ... Aha! Found it. *Faith* ... hm, a strange definition. Isn't that religion? Faith and religion are the same,' you think. 'I'm not a believer, I don't know what religion is and don't even dream of going to church,' you say to yourself. You close those dusty folders; some people even destroy them. No more faith, and no religion, whatever it means. Ultimately, some wise thought will appear on the front page and give you the answer you want because logarithms are wiser than the wisest sage today.

Where were we? Oh yes. Term deleted. Now you have space for new terms and thoughts. You can save memory – there's no need to remember any more.

11. 11 Love

I love you. Do you realise that? I miss you. I want to see you, hug you and speak some words you know very well but haven't heard from me in a long while ... probably never. I regret that. You deserve much better than a shabby departure with even shabbier words – goodbye, take care or something like that. I'm leaving, I'm coming, you're looking forward to me, I love you, you're here for me, I'm here for you, you love me, I'm looking forward to you. Poetry ...

I see you somewhere in the distance and don't have the strength to say anything. You're leaving, I'm leaving. 'See you in eight years,' I say. A lump in my throat ... I fear I'll never see you again, I fear I'll miss you for the rest of my life – or worse, we'll miss each other. We'll love each other secretly, like today, each of us in front of our computer screen, like eight years ago. Yes, I miss you. I've told you that already. I miss your voice, the quirky walks and drives, your laugh, and even your panic attacks. My heart aches when I think of you, when I remember. I try to understand what happened, and I try to understand myself. This world is strange – so small, yet so big. I came here to be alone. It's almost impossible. So much is unclear, nebulous, inarticulate. I love you. Have I told you that yet? I don't have the courage to turn up at your door, before your eyes, in front of you. Have I ever told you how wonderful you are sometimes? And how strenuous you can be; and how much I enjoy conversations with you. I haven't? Of course I haven't ... I'm terrified by the very thought that you could be the one – the one I've been dreaming of all these years ...

Never mind. I'm alive, and breathing, and writing. And I love. I eat little and sleep even less. Am I the only person who enjoys melancholy? The answer doesn't overly interest me.

12. 11 Hope

What is it that frustrates you? What is it that hurts? Ignorance. Ignorance hurts me, as do my brainwashed mind, every wound in my soul, every piece of flesh along with the glass in my heart. Every dark thought, every grey wall and every masked face hurts. I'm hurt by failure, which I don't see as such, but debased minds pressure me to see the world through their prism, to adopt their rules of existence, to reject myself and accept their illusion. But I forgive them. They do not know.

It hurts me that love has become just a trite term from the vocabulary of obscure romantics, and the way it's viewed by many who get lost in the mathematics of the rat race. Yes, even mathematics has become a worthless, laundered theory in its attempt to give value to worthless promises that will never be fulfilled. It all boils down to a deal with the devil, where he grins in disappointment and nods – souls are on discount today.

How much does one sincere embrace cost? How much an honest word and constructive criticism? 'Work on yourselves!' comes a shout from the crowd. 'We're working on ourselves, and enlightenment is just around the corner. Join us!' they go on, while our time trickles away. 'Can you make time stop?' I ask them, 'Kiss. Hours and minutes melt away, and you'll realise they never existed. Open yourself to love, and you'll realise pain never existed. There's only this immeasurable moment.'

I observe the lights of the city in the semi-darkness. People are chatting about trivia. It's the end of the working day and the beginning of free time. They used to call it leisure time. Hanging out at a bar. It seems boring at first glance. Such an ordinary form of communication, such a deadpan form of conversation. What would happen if I stood up and shouted: 'Let's kiss!' How many would start kissing there and then? All the conditions would be ripe: comfortable seats, soft music, the opposite or the same sex, a live broadcast of a match on a huge screen and a fantastic view of the city that seems to say, 'Kiss each other, dear people'... Everything is there, yet there are no kisses. I feel sorry for a young generation guided by just one slogan: Y*ou only live once*. Are you really alive?

Ideas come to us from time to time. We ignore them. We don't appreciate them; or don't appreciate them enough.

What would we give now for a clear mind and inspiration. Yes, yes, I can hear you. I hear the echo of your ego going on about your personal illusion because everyone has one in addition to the collective delusion. And no, I'm not going to bother with theories and definitions; there's Wikipedia if you want more information. This text is a mirror of your state of mind. Everything is just your projection. Do you have time for a few more sentences between scrolling? Still, love is not there.

We poison ourselves or allow ourselves to be poisoned – we don't know which. Poisons degrade the personality, addle the mind and destroy beauty. Who is responsible? But we waste time and energy if we search for the culprit. Let's take responsibility and move on. It hurts. But the pain is transient.

Bow, say thank you and smile – the curtain falls.

Zvonka Gazivoda

SOMETHING, AT LEAST

A two-storey house, unfinished. It's been like this for some time. A grey phase. Grey rendering. Grey day. Afternoon, early November, with the light fading. Grey. Maybe a watchman patrols the place, but there's nobody at the moment. Just three or four idlers and Bambi. They piled into the car and came from the city. It's not far.

Reinforcement wire leans near the entrance. A concrete mixer stands next to a tap and, a little further away, a stack of roof tiles – probably left over because the roof is finished. It's bound so it can't be stolen, or not so easily. They could at least have put an oilcloth over it, Bambi thinks, and then she remembers all the roofs in the world that have been leaking for years. She doesn't like to seem stupid, even if it's only to herself.

The group goes inside. Bambi barely knows them. They got together along the way and now she wonders whether to start talking with one of them or to look around the place. It's chilly and she's afraid of catching a cold. Today isn't the best day for the ballet flats she's wearing. Thin soles. The floor is concreted in places and elsewhere is still dirt. It's getting darker. Openings left for windows and doors gape between rendered bricks. The last straggling remnants of daylight seep through, ready to be cut short at any moment.

There's another girl in the group, she looks malnourished and is younger than Bambi. Her collarbones are like two stranded boats. As if sneaking away, Bambi goes for a walk around. No one pays attention to her. They sit on plastic barrels and talk. And spit. A bottle makes the rounds. Bambi can no longer make out words. She sees only the outlines of their figures.

The building has quite a square footage. A brick partition, possibly a future bar, separates a larger rectangular space from a smaller one; a connection between kitchen and dining room. Further inside, in a small room still to be rendered, stands a new toilet bowl. Not yet installed and without a cistern, it looks like a small spaceship. In the corner – workboots. The sewerage isn't finished, nor any of the sanitary facilities. She needs to pee. She walks and tightens the muscles of her pelvic floor, and also gathers her skirt so it doesn't sway. To keep a bit warmer.

The next space is large enough to fit two bedrooms. She comes across a long corridor. It seems there are to be office doors on the walls opposite. An unnecessary waste of space. She goes in and out – maybe these people are making a maze? Sandbags, boards, cigarette butts, stacks of tiles and screw stuff. (Where did she get 'screw stuff' from?) In some places, wires for electricity and light bulbs jut out.

Moisture is in the air and clings to the lungs. Bambi coughs a little as she inhales the smell of wet cement.

The strange need when walking for the hand to touch and pass over a rough wall, a hedge, a railing …

She's walked full circle and is now back at the beginning. She didn't go upstairs. She goes up to the others. Bambi only knows one of them by name, actually a nickname based on his prominent cheekbones and sunken eyes. Another is holding a crack bong, and the other girl is swigging from the bottle. All of them are strangely fidgety. They only exchange a few words. One of them laughs and then coughs. They shuffle from foot to foot or scrape a shoe on the floor like a horse with worn-out hoofs. The dust and their warm breath seem to make a mist hover between Bambi and them. She goes up close and smiles.

There's one now who wasn't there a moment ago. Shorter than Bambi. He comes towards her and Bambi holds out her hand, but he just grabs her upper arm and wants to drag her away. She resists half-heartedly and looks around in wonder, but her friends are busy with themselves – fixing their hair, brushing their sleeves or buttoning up – and now they go for a walk around the house. Skull remains, fortunately, but he goes to the window opening and lights a cigarette. It's as if smoking is prohibited inside, so he won't break the rules. He looks out and doesn't turn round.

Rain is pouring steadily.

Bambi struggles to get away. She props her foot against a doorframe, turns her back and pulls more strongly. One of her ballet flats falls off in the process, and the back of her head bashes the small stocky guy in the nose, accidentally, but so hard that he instinctively reaches for it with both hands. Bambi seizes the chance and breaks away. As she runs, she kicks a metal bucket, which spills lime, and then she trips over a wheelbarrow and stumbles, but manages to get up and escape from the hall.

She's already been through the whole house once, but that doesn't help her much. The layout of the rooms seems to have changed. Her own panting echoes in her ears, so she doesn't know if the guy is pursuing. She runs and searches for an opening in the wall to squeeze out through but ends up in the future bathroom. A dead end! A dead room! She gets up on top of the toilet, reaches for the small window opening high up in the wall and starts climbing. The veins on her neck are as thick as tendons, but she doesn't have the strength to pull herself up. She slides down and scratches herself, skinning her hands and knees, and tearing her tights. (It's been ages since she's worn those extra-thin ones.) She sits down on the toilet for a moment to catch her breath, when she sees her *friends* coming. One is pushing the wheelbarrow she fell over. Bambi grabs a bottle of paint thinner from the floor and looks for a plastic lighter, because if there are cigarette ends there must be a lighter somewhere, too. Let all of us burn! But she can't find one. She's ready to swing the bottle and hit the first person who comes near her or splash thinner in their eyes.

Although it's already as dark as pitch, she can see them frowning, wringing their hands and shaking their heads. The stocky guy, whose grip has left a mark on her arm, isn't with them. They slowly come closer, walking but stooped, and they seem to be looking past her. Bambi takes the opportunity to slip aside and get at them from behind. The skinny girl screams.

The toilet almost overflowed. It's full of red water. A haemorrhage. An abortion. Stirred red tempera. Bambi sweats, feels sick and grabs between her legs in panic. Then she notices the commotion of the friends. They give each other a leg up and crawl out through the window that was unreachable for her just a moment before. In the end, Skull is hanging upside down, the others outside are holding him by the legs, and he pulls up the girl, who is last. Light and as thin as shoelace, he hauls her out with no trouble.

Bambi is now all on her own. She turns abruptly towards the doorframe and faces the darkness. The whole house, which until then had neither doors nor windows, suddenly seems boarded up so that not a hint of darkness can enter, let alone light. She feels she's not alone. A faint scratching sound comes and confirms her fear. Like someone sanding wood with fine-grained emery paper. And maybe whistling at the same time. Or is she just imagining it?

Bambi takes a step back and presses her shoulders into the rough brick wall, but now she has nowhere to go. She looks up at the small window in despair.

All she wants is out.

She slips her hand into her tights as if squeezing her soft parts will give her security. She remembers to check her hand. It's dry – not a drop of blood.

That's something, at least.

Svetlana Kalezić-Radonjić

THE TITLE

The book she'd been working on so devotedly was finally finished. It had actually been written inside, long, long before, but it took time to lend it the most accurate form, close to that strange mixture of feelings that stirred in the depths of her being every time the thought of it arose. And she'd long dreamed of the Book while delaying its inception and fulfilling the tasks that were expected: finish her studies; get a job; marry; have children; hone her qualifications; get ahead, ahead, ahead.

Her long search for a title was finally over. The final step was now to get *her* blessing. She wasn't exactly a mummy's girl. Or rather, she was, but not as one might think at first glance. She loved her imperfect mother – who was at once gentle and rough, sublime and primitive, generous and selfish, and truly noble – in much the same way as one loves a sick child; with a love that is silent, sad, deep, all-encompassing and all-forgiving. Now she needed the same from her.

She put off talking to her all morning by inventing obligations – the unimportant and invisible ones that irrevocably turn life into a bacchanalia of banality: go shopping; hang up the washing; put on a new round of washing; fold the washing (fortunately she's so emancipated that she no longer irons[!] but buys crease-proof clothing); put away the toys; make the beds; put on lunch; dust; call the electrician about the light that hasn't been working for a year; call the plumber about the tap above the bath, which has had a life of its own for the past three months (dispensing water when no one turns it on and going dry when you want a gush); answer emails. When all the people she hadn't contacted for ages entered her mind and she thought now was the right time, there could be no more delay.

She called her mother. Her heart pounded in her ears and the sound of the phone made it syncopate.

'Mum, is that you? Have you read the book?' she got straight to the point.

'Hello, darling! I have – it's excellent!' came the reply without hesitation.

'Does anything need changing?' she trembled as she tried to sound disinterested.

'Tidy the text up a bit here and there, otherwise it's really great! It's obvious that you've been tied to the house and children so much in recent years because your sentence structure flags a little: you use too many catchwords, demonstratives, and the like ... but those are minor quibbles,' her mother said, noticeably proud of both her and the book, and unable to conceal that her retired professor's eye was still sharp.

'You're right, I've noticed that myself. I'll make those corrections. Could you return the manuscript? It's the only printed copy I've got.'

'I gave it to Ana to take to you. She should be there in the next twenty minutes. Have you decided on a title?'

'I have.'

'And?'

Svetlana Kalezić-Radonjić

'Well, I don't think you'll like it, but I can't let it go.'

'Hm. And what is it?'

An awkward silence unfolded.

Dense.

Sodden.

Sticky.

'*The Gospel of Clitoris*,' she finally spoke after the pause.

'That would be the end of me! There's no way you can call the book that!' her mother cried out in a voice of authority.

'But you don't understand – that's the only possible title,' she mounted a feeble attempt at defence. 'The book talks exclusively about women, about women's lives from the perspective of the female body, female sensitivity and female way of thinking. And which organ is the sublimation of everything female? Only the one that men don't have!'

'So you'd really do that to *us*?' her mother replied in a voice both deep and shrill, which heralded the end of the world.

'Do what, Mother, and how do you mean *us*?'

It had started.

A complex three-part composition. A-B-A.

A drama in two voices. For four hands.

A dour Montenegrin minuet.

'So the daughter of a famous father, the granddaughter of a celebrated Partisan, later a national hero, a descendant of prominent, honourable, modest and honest ancestors, would be so low as to name her book after the rudimentary penis women have as a ludicrous reminder of their potential power?'

'I can't believe what I'm hearing! Now you're playing the family-disgrace card if I call the book what I planned! And by the way, if Dad were alive he'd support me!'

'This is not America, this is not France, this is not Sweden! And you didn't know your father very well! This country has its own way of functioning, its own code of conduct, and if you haven't twigged by now you're a bigger fool than I thought! Here your life belongs above all to your ancestors and descendants, and only then to you!' the banner waved at the front line of the offensive, with the sound of a bomb accentuating the closing words.

'Do you really think I'd decide on something as crucial as the title without long, thorough consideration?'

'I know you wouldn't, so I'm all the more amazed you thought of calling the book *The Gospel of Clitoris*! The Church will come down on you like a ton of bricks and all the local Christians will foam at the mouth at such an insult! They'll crucify you!'

'Like a female Christ!' she tried to defend herself with irony and laughed.

'Go ahead, and then I'll hear: "Oh, Mother, help"!' the deep, angry voice persisted.

'Now I feel like burning the book,' the daughter said with a final wave of expiring life force.

Then silence. They both gulped audibly, a lump in their throats. They were breathing hard. The mother was the first to interrupt the alternating sighs.

'Listen ... Let's not be hasty. Put it aside for a few days, and then we'll talk about the title again. OK?'

'I've already had this conversation in my head several times, and it went exactly like this, with me even visualising a whole army of ancestors springing from their graves at your call, standing over me and shouting: "Boooo, clitoris!"'

At that moment, the mother made her famous Tao-manoeuvre.

48   Svetlana Kalezić-Radonjić

'Alright, darling, if you know what's best, then do what you think is right. You won't heed my word, so you're beyond my help.'

So that's how far it had got. The wisdom of doing nothing. A time-honoured trick that had her firmly in its sway. But it wouldn't work. Not this time.

'I've actually always heeded your word, but I can't say you're right now because your advice means haggling with art.'

'Do not talk to me of art!' The mother was evidently agitated, changed her intonation and began to rant. This happened every time her fundamental beliefs were challenged. In those moments, it was as if some great-great-great-ancestress leaped out of her, riding a warhorse, with her hair flying, her sabre aloft, ready to cleave off the first head that dared show itself above the parapet.

'You are a mother and the wife of a respectable man,' she continued. 'So you want people to point the finger at you and say, "There's the one who writes about the clitoris!"?'

'That's an argument your grandmother would have made a hundred years ago!'

'Don't be naive. In this country, some things will never change, regardless of innovations and progress! A good name is something you have to look after!'

'For God's sake, using the word "clitoris" in a title doesn't make me a whore!'

'Well, such are the times that it would be better for you to be a whore in hiding than to shout out a title like that in public, from hill to hill!'

The daughter couldn't take it any more. She hung up. Just then, Ana arrived with the manuscript.

She'd known for certain that the conversation would go like this and that her mother would prevail, even if she tried to oppose her. What she was up against was simply too strong.

It was time for her to finally grow up. But there's no growing up without rebellion. She'd correct the stylistic imperfections and send the final version to the publisher without relinquishing the title. That thought calmed and disquieted her at the same time. Although her mother was anachronistically modern, and although, alas, she was right about every piece of advice she gave, she, the daughter, felt with all her being that she had to persevere.

She fell asleep convinced of the correctness of her thoughts, but was woken up by the phone's insistent ringing.

What is it, this early?

It was her sister calling. 'Hello?' she spoke huskily.

'Mother's dead,' said a hoarse, heavy voice at the other end.

The phone fell out of her hand, which remained hanging in the air, and then rapidly fell apart as if made of sand.

She felt everything stop.

Time ceased to exist. Space was gone. The walls of the room were suddenly erased. She heard the voices of her family in the distance, but at that moment she couldn't remember how many children she had, if any. Hands were holding her shoulders and shaking her. Small crying faces were looking at her in fright. She couldn't feel her legs, only a strange numbness in her limbs that was mild enough so as not to remind her that her body existed. Her husband stared at her as if he was seeing her for the very first time, and then, with uncertain movements, he tried to usher the children out of the room with arguments none of them believed. They closed the door carefully, and despite the wooden barrier she could clearly hear their breathing, the thumping of their hearts and their feeling of powerlessness to say or do anything.

Svetlana Kalezić-Radonjić

And then it broke away. She'd once watched a documentary about a shaft inside Cheops' pyramid that the pharaoh's engineers constructed in order to lower three large granite blocks through it in the final stage of construction – the last defence of the King's Chamber that housed the sarcophagus. She'd wondered what that sound of finality might have been like. Now she knew – boooom, boooom, boooom!

Sealed forever.

When she slowly got to her feet, like in a silent film, she looked at the petrified faces of her family. No sound reached her. She sat down at the computer and located the manuscript of *The Gospel of Clitoris*. With the push of a button, just one button, everything was deleted. The same again in the Recycle bin.

The same way as everything was erased in her at that moment.

Slowly she went to the bookshelf and pulled out the only printed copy of the book written with such ardour. She took matches and a metal rubbish bin and went into the bathroom.

Earth to earth.

She put the manuscript in the bin.

Dust to dust.

She put the bin in the bath.

Fire to fire.

She burned the manuscript.

From nothing to nothing.

She watched the words burn that had been woven inside for years. She felt nothing.

The smoke wound upward in curls and flurries to touch the ceiling, steady and erratic at the same time, as if taunting it.

'All things are an exchange for *fire*, and *fire* for *all things*, as goods for gold and gold for goods,' droned the spirit of Heraclitus that suddenly appeared above her. 'This world-order, the *same for all*, no god nor man did create, but it ever was and is and will be: everlasting *fire*, kindling in measures and being quenched in measures,' he waffled on, his narrow nose flaring in bursts of self-satisfied respiration before each sentence. 'If all things were turned to *smoke*, the *nostrils* would distinguish them ...'

All of a sudden, there came a clatter of hooves in the distance. It grew ever louder as a strange rider approached. Finally she recognised her mother, who twisted in the saddle like a Mongolian archer, hauled up Heraclitus by his curly head and slung him bellyways over the horse.

'Silence, you fool, this is no time to philosophise! Everything of hers will be cindered!'

The old man fell silent, staring at the magnificent tail of the horse that rose up on its hind legs.

Her mother whipped around one last time – her hair flying in the wind in restless wisps, her eyes flashing warrior-like, *generalissima* of all the women from Eve onward. (Her strong arm still held Heraclitus so he wouldn't slide off when the horse reared.) She looked her straight in the eyes and smiled tenderly. Love overflowed in waves.

'I've always loved Chekhov,' she said momentously, emphasising the last word and spitting towards the unrepaired tap. And then, with a broad smile, she sped off in a cloud of dust.

And just as the flames were passionately caressing the paper, which changed colour as it curled, the faulty tap roared and shot out a stream of water that extinguished the burning manuscript. A small flame smouldered here and there, but there was no sign of the blaze that had raged just a moment earlier.

She looked into the bucket. Only the first two pages were destroyed. The title page and the one with the dedication. The rest had black marks around the edges, but the text was preserved.

With glowing eyes, she watched this birth.

Without any pain.

A long, slow birth.

The Gospel of Uterus.

Slađana Kavarić-Mandić

THE DAY
WITH THE HEAD

The day began normally. It would have been unusual if
we hadn't made love from 6.30 am. A disagreement about
who'd brew the coffee: I said I would because I sensed that
my man's insistence that he do it was a concealed reproach
about my coffee, and so the questioning fed itself; everyone
likes my coffee, but he finds fault with it, although he's
never verbalised that, just like many other things only I
thought should have been. The bedding was soon out in
the sun, the room could already have been someone else's,
aired and without the smells of our awakening. All rooms
are potentially someone else's and possibly no longer ours.
Between a mouthful and a sip of coffee, he said love is when
you'd die for someone. A platitude that needs to be thought
through and fleshed out. All truth is in general viewpoints
that are bypassed in hipster style while smart-arsing about
personal choices and alternative paths. As a man who loves
the whole world and embraces it with cringeworthy passion
like an adolescent does nonconformity, he's already died for
everyone. It was easy to want to die for me too when dying
is like that – more or less collective.

The hardest thing would be to throw myself under the
train, I thought. When I was six, a train stopped by my

house – the house closest to the track, and this was nothing unusual because trains broke down almost every day, and the sound of them screeching to a halt was common and familiar, but that day, unexpectedly, a man ran frantically into the yard from the direction of the railway; Dad said he was an engine driver and all I remember is my parents trying to calm him down – although it was hard to imagine anyone being calmed by my mother, who herself became anxious and maudlin at everything; the engine driver shouted that he misjudged – he thought the man was just going to wave as he passed, but he laid his head on the track. That was my first brush with suicide. Dad took a colourful bedsheet and went out towards the track. Later he said crows were already on the decapitated body, although I imagined them on the disembodied head. They'd peck at the dead eyes like a child eats jelly. The head was crushed into the rail, and a few metres away lay a hat on which the man had placed two stones, in order to point out, just in case, that it hadn't been an accident. I liked to muse about the symbolism of the two rocks, and in the following days I thought that the number of rocks must represent the number of reasons. If this visual message with the hat caught on, most people would pour a handful of sand into the hat because there are always too many reasons or, even better, I thought, it would be better to turn the hat over and put a big rock in it instead of a head and thus send a clear message – a weight replaced the head. And if you think with that gravity, with that one reason, your head no longer asks itself. It rushes to the tracks, deceives the engine driver – and forces him to see rolling heads, not wheels, for the rest of his life.

I didn't say anything about dying under a train. One dies for love more romantically – in a duel, on canvas or in words, but not in reality. And me, would I die for someone?

I wondered about that all day. I vacuumed the new carpet and thought about death. I'd never thought about it in this way before. My deaths were selfish and personal.

I'd wanted to kill myself when it got dark and was time to go home from the playground, when the teacher praised someone other than me, when my best friend told me the boy I had a crush on was in love with someone else, when the heroes of my favourite books killed themselves ... This later progressed to the suicides of friends and relatives, whose reasons were just as major as mine from childhood, because reasons are measured according to weight and height. The thought of the end has been there in its own way since that day – the day with the head and the train, ever since the sheet ended up on someone else's corpse instead of my bed. I went out onto the balcony of this house that knows no trains, next to my man, for whom trains are a symbol of studying in a city that's easiest and cheapest to reach by rail. Everyone went to Belgrade the first time by train, and I always felt sick in such trains, I muttered. I gathered up the bedclothes hanging over the balcony railing of our new flat. This evening was no longer the same as yesterday's, which had been the same as the previous ten, which we also ended here, on the balcony. I imagined for a moment that the view from the balcony was a view into the wheels of a train, and then I took the sheet and threw it down. May it serve for someone's head. No, we're not going to open a new bottle of wine tonight, OK?

Olja Knežević

TRAPPED

'I'm trapped,' he complained as soon as Magda entered the apartment.

'What? Didn't the babysitter come?' she asked.

'She did, but that's not the point,' he replied. 'I told her to go as soon as I got in. Ten pounds an hour for what? The meetings with your would-be writers are no longer necessary. You've finished postgraduate studies, so now it's an ordinary social gathering. You don't really care, I see.'

'Good night,' she said.

They parted at the end of the narrow corridor. Magda soon fell asleep beside her daughter.

At breakfast: 'This is not how I imagined life.'

At least I'll learn why he thinks he's trapped, Magda thought.

First, he reminded her that the windows in his office can't be opened.

I know, I know, Magda answered without a voice, nodding almost imperceptibly and opening her mouth like a fish on dry land.

'That way I can smell all the constituents of the recycled office air even better,' he went on with his moaning. 'Heavy metals, plus viruses and bacteria that keep mutating like hell. All that muck heads straight to the cerebral cortex. Not just mine – everyone's. But life is only for the clever, and most people aren't. People are absent and unaware; you don't see it because you don't go to work. People don't understand life and will never realise that that chemical cocktail is the main cause of the epidemic of depression, for example.'

His boss is an idiot savant like most of his fellow workers, he continued, except that this one is a fucking CEO and a real drunkard who torments him with his envy until noon, and after lunch maunders on about his hunting exploits, rendered incomprehensible due to his chronically inflamed sinuses and additionally clogged by the sulphates from the white wine.

'I told him he ought to have his sinuses checked, or switch to quality red wines,' her husband claimed. 'Imagine, he was offended. Everything's been handed to him on a platter since he was born. His starting position in life was set to plus one hundred, not like me; my life didn't start from zero but from minus one hundred. It's the same with you and everyone else from our region.'

'But still, they pay for your transport into the City, with the parking thrown in! Working hours from ten until you decide to knock off. Look at our relaxed breakfasts together, the paid restaurant bills, hotels, business-class travel, and bonuses – fantastic!' Magda effervesced.

Her husband didn't want to join in her joy. It scared him, because joy is a big wave, a vortex that carries everything away. One of the few stories that can cheer him up is a Jewish fable, and he sometimes asks her, 'Do you know the Jewish joke?' to which she never says 'yes', because he enjoys telling it – the one about a Brooklyn rabbi who always borrows a thousand dollars in cash before he sings. The

Olja Knežević

punchline: 'You sing better with a thousand dollars in your pocket.'

She should have killed her joy, donned a frowning mask, argued with him, or told him ten years ago to look after the children – he can do everything – so that she could go out and be among people, at least part-time. But she never did; he brought home a salary, and the one time he took the children to the park he had a nervous breakdown when the football with Thierry's signature got wedged up in a tall chestnut tree.

'Try to raise these children properly,' he admonished her after that aborted spree in the park. 'I thought they were different – that they had self-control.'

Before leaving for work, her husband tells her: 'You know, you don't have to strangle yourself with a tie and go to catch the train every morning. You don't have to eat in a canteen where they haven't even heard of wholemeal bread or cheese other than plasticky Cheddar, which makes my blood pressure rocket. You don't have to do any of that. The least you can do is care for these children properly. Your meetings with the group are now pure socialisation, not part of your studies anymore.'

Inside, but not aloud, Magda reminds him that he never takes the train or subway, and she doesn't share with him how magical she finds it that he can leave the apartment every morning and go somewhere where they pay him to use his brain, and in parallel to reflect and defend his conclusions. She envies his requirement to look good every day, in a jacket, coat or suit tailored to his figure. Dressing up for work and going to get paid to think Monday to Friday makes the weekends meaningful. Let it be that way, she concluded, let the children grow up with a mother. Their father is a hand sometimes clenched, sometimes generous.

She put on a dressing gown over comfortable pyjamas instead of a coat over a bodyhugging dress, and stayed in it for a year, three years, then five, ten ... Her husband believes that she is therefore free, while he is trapped.

*

'I'm taking you all out to dinner,' he said after work, stroked her hair, her back, and let his hand slide. 'Come on, stop tenderising those steaks. I really want to eat the dumplings at that restaurant tonight.'

But something slid downhill at the restaurant. That something was Magda. Her husband was tired, so why was she now an additional burden to him? He yelled at her in front of everyone when she nudged the remains of her black cod under her serviette because she thought it would make her sick.

'You're always absent,' he told her, not for the first time. 'You don't appreciate me, my money or my effort. That's you, always hiding something under a metaphorical serviette. Why don't you slink back to your hole?'

He pronounced that in a raised voice in front of *everyone* – guests and employees alike. And in front of the children, of course, but that didn't count any more. The children had grown up to the rhythm of ups and downs, and they'd survive. Other people secretly loved it, because they were witnessing a public lynching but without feeling primitive.

Her husband can't stand her inability to raise her voice, protest, tell the waiter that the black cod is undercooked and send it back. He says it's a waste of time and energy, and that it leads nowhere. For her, it's easier to stay a spoiled girl, play hide-and-seek and conceal the undercooked piece

Olja Knežević

of fish in her serviette. Framed in a particular picture, nailed to the chair in the restaurant, she can't send the food back with the waiters. She's soft on them; they, of course, ignore her in return.

He's right, Magda thinks. *They don't notice me at all, but they adore him. They admire his masculinity – he's masculine and handsome, and men like that are ever rarer in the world, while there are more and more masculine women.* The waiters call Magda's husband 'Mister B'. It seems the whole city calls him that now. Magda even heard some people say, *Mister B? B stands for Boss.* At the restaurant, everyone looks at him with admiration as he criticises them and teaches them their own job, and he competes with the sommeliers in his knowledge of wine, which they evidently enjoy. He's just sent back a few bottles of wine because the corks were compromised, he said, holding the corks under their noses. They smelled, bowed, and then probably spat on *Magda*'s food in a dark corner without a camera – she's sure of it – but not on *his* because they fear him.

She won't send back the fish. It's a small victory of her true nature, and she'll order alcohol to celebrate and get herself tipsy. She orders champagne, by the glass, and ends up ordering three glasses. Her husband tanks up on wine – they've finally been able to satisfy him. The kids are on their phones: they're well trained and don't ask when they'll be going home.

A graceful Chinese pianist soulfully renders new classic and jazz. Magda falls in love with the movements of his tiny fingers and the simple passion with which he loves his work. The pianist may not have even noticed her, and yet he sends her a message through the notes, to the gist that people like Magda and him have no nerve for quarrelling with waiters, but they always have time for small kindnesses like playing the piano in restaurants, usually for the one person it will mean something to, in a group that's come to talk, eat and drink. A tear rolls down her cheek, but only from the eye her husband can't see. He intently watches her profile and registers that she's overwhelmed by sentimentality. About what? If not about him, her husband, then perhaps it's that cowardly capitulation again to memories of their accursed common homeland. He could never guess that it's the tiny hands of the Chinese pianist doing what he loves and which no one has to pay for, either literally or figuratively. Her husband is intelligent but has no imagination. Oh, he could find someone much better than this nostalgic woman now, but what would he do with her? Still, she's a halfway decent refuge for his children, her routine is familiar, she doesn't cost him much and she has a good record of responding to calls.

'Magdalena! Magda! Hey, Magda!' he calls across the table, as if there's a roaring highway between them. And as he speaks to her and asks why now this and not that, she no longer understands him; she only sees and understands the mosquito that clings to the smooth skin of his cheek, where it tries to suck his blood. It tries and tries but can't get out a single drop. Finally defeated, and dead or near death, the mosquito falls from her husband's cheek and plops into his glass of wine.

Jelena Lengold

DO YOU REMEMBER ME?

Tomi decided on the spur of the moment to order another drink, although he didn't feel like it at all. Not that he'd felt like the first drink either, but it was always awkward for him to walk into a bar just to use the bathroom. And so he'd sit down at the bar like that, although he didn't like bars; he found them mostly uncomfortable, he didn't like drinking alone, didn't like short drinks, and he didn't like sultry summer evenings when the asphalt steams after an afternoon shower and it seems there's not a breath of fresh air anywhere. But this bar was pleasantly temperate and he thought that that, at least, made some sense. He'd cool down a bit, rattle the ice cubes and feel the beaded glass in his hand, stare at the orderly rows of bottles in front of him, and time would pass quickly. Then he'd leave.

But while Tomi was still on his first drink, he saw a woman watching him. When he dared to focus on her for a second or two, he thought she even smiled at him. The woman was sitting alone at her table. At first, he couldn't believe his eyes, but then, glancing sideways, furtively, once, a second time, then a third, he was convinced: she really was looking at him. Him! He didn't understand why.

No one had looked at him for a long time, be it on the street, at work, on the train he travelled to the office in every day, in waiting rooms or queuing at the post office – no one's eyes lingered on him. Tomi had been aware for years that he'd fallen irreversibly into the category of unremarkable people: he was of average height, average weight and average looks, with an average balding head and inconspicuous, uninteresting clothes. Even if he wished to, he wouldn't have been able to step out of his own character. He probably didn't even want to.

But this woman was looking at him, and although she wasn't an eye-catcher herself and couldn't be considered beautiful, and although she was a thoroughly inconspicuous and ordinary woman, whom he probably wouldn't have noticed in any other place, Tomi heard himself order that second drink. Then he turned just a little to the side on the high and uncomfortable bar stool so he could observe the woman more easily. Or so she could see him better. He thought that if she took a really good look at him, she'd realise there was nothing noteworthy about him. Yet when he turned and exposed the greater part of his face to her, he realised she'd placed both hands under her chin as if she wanted to take a more comfortable position from which to watch him. Strange, thought Tomi. The world was full of lonely, distrustful people. He'd been like that himself for some time, and certainly since his divorce. Why this woman didn't show that so recognisable and understandable mistrust is what confused him most. Yes, this time she really smiled at him. And, quite involuntarily, he smiled back. It was almost a reflex, like when you smile at a baby and it instinctively returns the smile. After the age of three or four, children stop smiling automatically at anyone who gives them a smile, they become cautious and remain that way forever. That's why he was surprised when he realised he was smiling broadly. A muscle in his cheek hurt, and he thought it must have been a long time since his face had last stretched into a smile like that.

Then everything happened quickly. The woman waved and motioned for him to come and sit next to her. He acted as if he wasn't sure she meant him and pointed at himself as if to ask, *me, really*? She smiled again and nodded. Just then, the barkeeper put the second drink down in front of him. Tomi took the glass and went over to the table where the unfamiliar woman was sitting.

'Do you remember me?' she asked as soon as he sat down, after looking him straight in the eyes for a few seconds.

Tomi was confused. He didn't remember her face or the hands holding the cup of coffee. Nor did he remember the thick locks of hair that fell in waves about her shoulders. He simply did not remember this woman. He shook his head, bewildered and uneasy.

'Do you really not remember me?' she continued, with the same smile, as if they'd begun playing a game in which he pretended not to recognise her, and she knew it couldn't possibly be true and let him dally a little longer.

'I'm afraid not,' Tomi admitted.

'I don't believe you,' she said, and her face grew a little serious – just the face, not the smiling eyes. 'You're kidding.'

'Not at all. This is actually embarrassing. What's your name?'

'I'm not going to tell you because I know you'll remember.'

Now Tomi finally smiled again.

'OK, but at least give me a hint. Where do we know each other from? When was it?'

'Not that long ago. You should remember unless you've had some kind of amnesia.'

'Maybe you're mixing me up with someone else. I'm Tomi …'

'Of course, I know full well who you are. Are you still married?'

'No, I've been divorced for five years. So, we met before that?'

'That's right,' the woman said and took a sip of her coffee.

She seemed very calm, as if she was still waiting for it to click with him. Tomi glanced furtively at his watch. It was Friday, and half past five in the afternoon. He had to pick up his son at seven. This was his weekend on. *I guess we'll figure out who's who by then*, he thought.

'Wait for me a minute,' the woman said and got up from the table.

As she walked away, Tomi watched her closely. She had good legs and firm, round hips. *How could I have forgotten? And what was between us anyway?* She'd looked at him a moment ago in a way that said just one thing: somewhere, sometime, at some point they'd shared a secret.

The woman came back, sat down and gently waved her wet hands to try and dry them. That movement reminded him of something, but what? She was silent, waiting for him to speak.

'Look,' Tomi said, 'apart from the first and maybe second year of my marriage, all the others were pretty chaotic. There were days and nights, especially nights, when I had no idea what to do with myself.'

'Are you saying you screwed a whole load of women back then – so many that you've forgotten the odd one?'

'No, no I didn't. Or I did, but not so many that I'd forget.'

'Hm.'

'Does that mean that you and I ...?'

She nodded.

'How many times?'

The woman just gave a thumbs-up. That presumably meant once. Tomi wasn't surprised – scarcely anything he did in those years went beyond one meeting. One desperate attempt to touch another human being. Then he'd usually leave, even more desperate and placated only in the most remote part of his being. Everything beyond that still trembled with anxiety and impotence.

Maybe I should try a joke, Tomi thought.

'And how was it?'

'Fair to middling,' the woman said and twirled her hand again. 'You were nervous. And quiet. Just like now.'

'I'm not nervous now, just confused. This is incomprehensible to me.'

'Not to me.'

'What are you getting at?'

'People suppress things that get under their skin. It's normal.'

'What got under mine?'

The woman leaned on her elbows and looked at him again, now a little more seriously.

'Hang on, Tomi, is this for real? Are you saying you really don't remember all that? Nothing?'

Tomi shook his head and spread his arms helplessly. He needed another drink. He tried to catch the barkeeper's eye.

'At least tell me your name.'

'A name doesn't matter if you don't remember anything,' the woman said. 'How many other women did you sleep with while you were married?'

'Not many. Four or five, six at most. And I'm convinced I remember each of them well.'

'Well, that's not how it seems.'

'It's not many for twelve years in that state.'

'You don't have to justify yourself to me. Then again, if you don't remember me this whole conversation makes no sense. It's best I go.'

She got up and took her handbag from the chair. Tomi got up too. He didn't know what to say.

'Goodbye,' the woman said, turned away and headed for the exit.

That word, *goodbye*, struck him in the plexus. The day he left his house, wife and child, long ago, Tomi promised himself he'd never take another goodbye, even if it meant being alone forever. With two steps he reached the bar, paid, and dashed out. The heat hit him in the face as he tried to see which way the woman had gone. She almost eluded him in the direction where the low early evening sun blinded the passers-by. But he recognised the legs and hips, and hurried after her.

'Wait,' he called at the next corner, as he caught up.

The woman stopped and looked back. She didn't seem at all surprised.

'Now what?' she asked. 'Do you remember?'

'No, but I don't want it to end like this. You have to tell me. Everything.'

The woman sighed, with a hint of impatience.

'It's so hot. And besides, why should I tell you what you obviously wanted to forget?'

'But what? I don't understand what I've forgotten. Please don't go. Tell me when we met, how we met and what happened.'

The woman searched for something in her handbag, then took out a large clasp and raised her hair. *I know that move too*, Tomi thought. *I know that neck, yes.*

'There's no need for me to tell you everything,' the woman said, wiping her neck under the hair with the flat of her hand. 'I'll tell you just this: before we parted, you told me, "For the first time in ten years I feel I'm alive." Then you left and I never heard from you again. And today you don't remember me.'

She turned away from him again, this time without saying goodbye, and almost ran across the street. She began to disappear in the mass of people on the pavement opposite.

For a few moments he went completely stiff, all his senses numbed, and then he suddenly realised that he mustn't lose her. He crossed the street and took up pursuit.

She walked fast, so following her was difficult. The sun beat down on his forehead. He panted. Several times he worried because he couldn't see her, but then a lock of her raised hair would flutter again among the people, cars and traffic lights. Once she stopped in front of a shop window and once at a kiosk, where she bought something – just long enough for Tomi to catch his breath and continue after her. It was already six twenty, and he was chasing an unknown woman in a direction completely opposite to the one he should have been going. *Please, please go into one of the buildings and show me where you live*, Tomi thought. *Show me who you are and I'll never forget you again.*

As if she heard him, the woman suddenly stopped in front of a building and opened her handbag. She took out a key. Then she unlocked the door and entered. That was it. Now he knew where she lived. He waited a minute so she had time to go where she was going, and then he approached the entrance. He looked at the surnames on the nameplate. None of them rang a bell. He stood there, not knowing what to do next. Then he looked at his watch again. Half past six. He simply had to go and pick up his son if he was to get there on time; he didn't want to face the music for being late again.

He turned his back to the sun and hurried, now in the opposite direction.

When he finally put his son to bed around ten that evening, he opened a beer and sat out on the balcony. He caught himself smiling as he thought back to the movement as she raised her hair and revealed her delicate neck.

On Saturday, he and his son played chess almost all day outside under the large linden that grew right next to the window of his flat. The boy preferred spending time with his father to playing with other children. Several times he intentionally let the boy win, but once he made a gross oversight and was immediately forced to concede the game. The boy squealed with pleasure and happily slurped his juice through a straw. Tomi had been thinking of those fast, slender calf muscles running across the street.

On Sunday evening, alone in his flat again, he realised he had a burning desire to return to that building. But what would he say to her, even if she did appear? He didn't know. He sat up until midnight thinking about it. And then, in those few moments before sleep took him, he suddenly knew what he had to say: *I haven't forgotten you. How could I ever forget you? I've forgotten myself. Please forgive me.*

He waited outside her building on Monday night. And on Tuesday. And on Wednesday. He felt he knew all the people who lived there by heart. By now he feared she'd never show up, or that he was maybe standing in front of the wrong building, or that she'd just gone to visit someone and didn't actually live there. *Or did I make everything up? Did I perhaps never meet her at all?*

And then she suddenly appeared. Before he realised it was really her – this time in tight white pants and a red T-shirt open at the back, and he took her in and let her pass through his senses – she was a good hundred metres away. He set off after her like a stalker, not even knowing why he was secretly following her, and why he didn't just hurry and go up to her. But something about her walk and her pace was irresistible to watch. The handbag over her shoulder swung in the same rhythm as her hair, which was tied back into a ponytail. *She was absolutely right*, Tomi thought – *I feel alive! I once forgot what it was like to be alive, but that mustn't happen again.* In his mind, his hand was already moving gently from her soft elbows to her shoulders. *She was mine before and she'll be mine again. All of her. This swaying. I'll explain it to her and she'll come back to me.*

She stopped to wait for a bus. Tomi stopped too, hidden behind a billboard. Two buses passed, and she didn't get on. He feared she'd disappear into the crowd that was constantly forming at the stop. Then a third bus came. He realised she intended to get on this time. He waited for her to go up the steps and squeeze in among the people, and, a second before the bus doors closed, he got in too.

He slowly forced his way through the throng and tried to get close to her. He didn't know what he should do – speak to her there in the bus or just watch her. The situation had become so absurd that it even amused him a little. The woman's back was turned to him. She was holding onto a bar with one hand and tightly clutching her handbag under her other arm. Now he could smell her hair. He was right behind her. Stiff and hardly breathing, he was afraid she might suddenly turn around and see him. And yet a part of him seemed to want exactly that. He didn't know what he really wanted. He realised he hadn't even seen which bus he got into and where the line went. *Where am I actually going?*

Opposite her stood a man. They were holding on to the same bar. He was tall, with a moustache and the serious face of someone who never hesitates. Tomi avoided his gaze. He tried to look only at her hair and keep imbibing that scent until something – anything – happened. *This is it! I'm going after her. It doesn't matter where. All that matters is that I follow her.*

And then something really did happen. She slowly raised her head, waved her hair, and he clearly heard her speak the words to that stern gaze opposite:

'Do you remember me?'

Ana Miloš

PEACE

Srđan died. The tiny body that had been him was now a cold and motionless pile of something. There was no scene in which frantic medical workers race into the patient's room and, with expressions of sympathy and compassionate anguish, strive to turn the straight line on the ever-green monitor into a zigzag that joyfully beeps life. I let him lie. I imagined his soul passing out through his nose and kissing him on the forehead before flying away. I imagined him falling through a burn-hole at the end of the bed and sliding into the netherworld. I was interrupted by a young woman in a white uniform. She wanted to know if everything was OK. I nodded. I was frightened of all the bureaucracy the little cadaver would entail. I wanted to run away.

I got up and went to his tiny nose and slightly parted lips. From them – silence. I caressed his head, and his hair fell on his temples and forehead like cut grass. I felt an urge to just leave, but I knew I couldn't. My tears started as soon as I went out into the green-and-cream laminate corridor, looking for a nurse and muttering the ultimate statement. In the maze of wandering patients, clumsy clogs and morbid wheelchairs, I found her. My tears, inflamed eyes and flushed face were enough of a cue.

She shouted something, and then the doctor came running into the room, forever late and unnecessary. They confirmed the death, expressed their condolences, and took the little boy away on the bed where he died.

I needed to go down to the morgue.

We all cried at the cemetery. They say the worst thing is when a child dies. When an old person passes away it doesn't matter because they've lived a long life. But when potential dies, it's a disaster. I think every life is equally valuable or none are. We should agree about that once and for all.

Finally alone. No more phone calls, internet messages or telegrams (I didn't know the human race still uses them, but when the postman knocked and handed me a condolence note I had to change my mind). No more relatives and friends insisting on being there, by my side, to help. Everything fell silent. Not even him shouting from the next room or calling me from the hospital. With demands. There was nothing else, it seemed, except me. That thought lifted my spirits so much that I smiled and then laughed. My laughter echoed through the empty space as if the flat was condemning me. I calmed down, glanced around needlessly and went out onto the small balcony.

I'd always wanted to have a small table and a barstool there so I could drink morning coffee looking out over the rows of low houses, with their roofs of desire lines for cats, their mouths of chimneys, treetops and people.

The nearest furniture store is a twenty-minute walk from my flat. I sold the car when Srđan had to go into hospital. The neighbour who lives in the flat below mine has a car, and as far as I know he's unemployed – he had to help me.

He was ready in a flash as if he'd just been waiting for my call. We hopped in the car, parked in the shopping centre, entered the store and inspected the chairs. We chatted and walked along past the furniture and household goods. He liked my idea.

'I exercise on the balcony. I love it there, even in winter. It's too small for push-ups, but I can lift dumbbells and do squats.'

I imagined him in his boxers, sweaty and tense.

'Better take two barstools. Then you can have coffee with someone else.'

No one had made a pass on me for a long time, so his directness made me blush.

Still, I just took the one.

My neighbour assembled it and carried it out onto the balcony. The table I liked had been the only one in the shop, so I took it as it was. The furniture now meant there was barely room for me on the balcony, let alone for him. We were sardined on that concrete slab and hemmed in by the metal railing, so we had no choice but to rub against each other. He must have been experienced because he didn't lose a second; he gently clasped my waist, glanced into my eyes, smiled and kissed my cheek. He separated from me just enough to be able to beam at me amorously, then he descended on my lips and stayed there until they parted and let him in.

He could have screwed me there on the balcony, but inhibition was stronger than desire, so we moved to the room and the sofa. We didn't take off our clothes. We squeezed and ground against each other. We trembled. He was inside me, hard and filling, and I was wet, wet. Like kids doing a quickie. We paused, drank some juice, then I folded out the couch, took my clothes off, took off his, and we fucked in peace, long and good.

We chattered again, holding each other loosely, still sweating and panting. It was warm outside, late May – perfect weather. I would have liked to go for a jog. I'd had enough of the dick. But he didn't leave. *Never mind*, I thought, *he's funny*.

He asked who it was in the photo near the TV. I told him it was my recently deceased son. He stiffened and cooled down in an instant. He got up and dressed.

'Sorry, I didn't know. I didn't see the death notice.'

'I didn't put one up.'

He cursed me and muttered. I asked him to say it again, but that infuriated him; he swore and berated me as if I were a child. Then he left and slammed the door.

Milan had been calling me for days. He'd only seen Srđan rarely, maybe once a month. He paid maintenance, and I was grateful for that. Otherwise he left us alone. He didn't make scenes. His unbounded obstinacy and selfishness were easily silenced by hanging up. After a long ring, I opened the door to see him hopping and spinning around on the mat, as if trying to see something clinging to his back.

'You don't answer the phone. I had to come like this. We need to talk.'

I didn't see why, or about what, but I let him in. I didn't offer him anything to drink in the hope that he'd leave sooner rather than later. But he sat down in the armchair, glared around, ordered a coffee and went up to Srđan's photo on the shelf near the TV. He took the frame and raised it to his glasses. He touched the picture, ran his little finger over the glass and showed me the grey on the tip.

'You don't even take care of yourself.'

I stood with my arms crossed, at contrapposto, and rolled my eyes. I demanded he put the photo back and say what he wanted.

'I was at the cemetery. The grave is totally neglected.'

He continued in that vein: he was constantly on the road, often teaching abroad; as Srđan's mother, I should take care of the grave; if that was too much of an obligation for me, he'd pay someone to do it; he didn't understand how I could be so selfish, how I could not care.

He was so tedious that I stopped listening to him; I reduced him to a bout of tinnitus and waited for another noise to overlap him and drown him out. After an endless monologue he noticed I was ignoring him, so he pounded his fists and demanded attention.

'You are a vile person!'

He fled in the end, forgetting that he still held the dusty photo in his hand. I locked the door. I hoped he wouldn't give it back out of spite – that that was it and we wouldn't see each other again.

And we didn't. It must have been a year after his sermon. He sent me a message that he'd hired an old man who cleaned at the cemetery. He didn't write that I should pay, so I didn't even answer.

My neighbour decided not to talk to me any more, despite us having had good sex; Srđan affects me even from the grave. But since there are men everywhere, I don't miss him much. Jogging and a good diet make me attractive. I've always had good looks. I spend my salary just on myself, so I've got a good wardrobe. I barely recognise myself in the mirror – the new me takes some getting used to.

The anniversary of Srđan's death is the only day in the year I think of him. The date, hour and minute are engraved in my brain and I can't go against those memories. Instead of suppressing them and agonising, I let them out. I make a place for them in my new life every year and browse with joy through the old photos: from school, from summer and winter holidays, when he was little in a baby walker, at grandma and grandpa's ... That day is for him and me. I switch off. Him and me again. I even cry, but I never go to the cemetery.

Then one day I went to the cemetery. I'd been thinking about it for days and in the end I caved in – you have to cater to your weaknesses. Six years had passed, so I wandered among the tombstones and wooden crosses for a long time. I couldn't find Srđan's grave. But I'd set out to clean it, so clean it I would.

The old man whom Milan hired was either dead or taking the money and doing nothing. Everything was covered in dust, bird droppings, fallen leaves, mud and cigarette butts. The marble was dirty, and the earth around the grave itself looked fresh as if people had been standing and grieving, and I could see shoeprints.

I put the canvas bag down on the ground, crouched and took out the gardening gloves with rubber pimples on the fingers. I tore out the weeds and cleaned the lumps of soil off the slab and around it. I took a plastic bottle out of the bag, filled it with water at the next tap, and sprinkled the whole grave. I took two cloths and wiped down the marble. I needed another bottle to make the slab and the gravestone shine. I took a third, clean cloth and wiped everything meticulously so the heat wouldn't leave amoeboid traces of limescale. I had a small broom with me too, so I tried to clean away as much as possible of the mud that had spread around the grave. But that raised dust, so I went to the tap once more, and again I poured, rubbed, washed and wiped.

In the end, everything was spick and span.

I wanted to be completely alone and didn't bring my mobile, so I didn't know what time it was. There was no one to be seen at the cemetery. The sun was getting lower and lower. It must have been at least two hours since I'd arrived.

I packed everything into the bag and headed for the exit. The pressure in my bladder was unbearable. I looked around. I wondered if there was a toilet at the chapel, but even then I didn't have time. I hobbled behind a big tree, as if hiding from myself. The bag and my panties went down in one movement, and I lifted my skirt. A stream shot out. I held on to the tree with both hands. Two red beetles bumbled over the bark, connected in a mating dance. They were droll because they kept stumbling on the rough bark. My stream weakened and disappeared. Relief, at last.

Katarina Mitrović

SMALL DEATH

Fear of being left alone. Fear that everyone I love will die. Fear that I'll never have children. Fear that if I do, they'll hate me for having them and hurry to leave me. Fear of black, of burial places and of no one wanting to touch me. Fear because I'm thirty and haven't done what's expected of me. If I don't do something, everyone will give up on me. Fear of everyone giving up on me.

And also the fear that I'm a bad person because I'm never on time, don't honour agreements and don't answer the phone. I forget my best friends' birthdays and buy stupid gifts. I'm selfish, always wanting something. I expect others to anticipate how I feel. I think there are at least five people who'd like to slap me in the face. My fits of rage are a story in themselves. I yell at my mother and manipulate lovers. I lie. I lie even when I don't have to, and especially when I don't want to. I think too highly of myself and ridicule what I don't understand. When I lose my temper I get the urge to bash my head against the wall. I'm a cheater. I dance drunk around the house. I'm unlucky in love. I blame others for everything. I haven't finished uni. I don't have children, although I've had many opportunities to. I've ruined all my relationships. The people I've been with definitely have all manner of bad things to say about me, and they probably do. Fear of living.

I tried to force my teeth, tongue, velum and lips to speak all these words so this guy would immediately realise who I am. Maybe then he'd be honest too and we wouldn't waste years pretending. I really try, but then I hear myself say:

'Fuck talking. Want to swim?'

The sand was hot and I'd left my flip-flops back at the tent, so I had to run to the water. He ran too, not because he couldn't stand his soles burning but because he thought it was a game. Like in the movies when they suddenly take off and jump into the water.

But I couldn't just jump straight in the water because it was cold and I wanted to get a little wet first. That already revealed a lot about me. I looked down and judged my bikini. I wasn't satisfied. It had looked much better in the cabin, and it seemed that the mirror there created the impression of thinness, and only now did I realise that it was see-through when wet. My nipples were visible and erect from the cold. I think he liked it, but I was embarrassed, so I decided to go all the way in as soon as I could and hide my body underwater.

He didn't want to go in deep and I couldn't detect if he was afraid. The water on Ada Bojana is very shallow and we could have walked out for kilometres, but the waves were getting bigger and bigger, pushing us towards each other, then away from each other. We were both goosepimply, bristly and edgy, as if we'd been thrown to an animal that spat us out and then ate us all over again. I was a little scared, but the excitement prevailed when he told me he'd fallen in love. I felt the same way. It didn't matter that we'd only just met. That really wasn't important. I'd already waited too long and couldn't take it any more. I think others would have been happy for me too.

I ran my hand from his muscular biceps to his bony fingers. I felt tiny notches in his skin as if he had scars. I liked that. He was a real, capable man and couldn't take his eyes off me. That's what he told me.

When we got out of the water, I ran to the car to change, and he went to get beer. I raised my wet bottom and put a towel under me, found a dry bathing suit and pulled it on. Through the window I saw a cat bounding away across the parking lot. It was extremely small and thin, but agile and playful, falling and rolling after every leap. I opened the door and it started to wind itself around my legs.

In the distance, I saw my girlfriends pitching a tent. They laughed loudly and teased me because of Balša (that was his name). I went back with the cat in my arms. It snuggled up to me the whole time and poked its nose into my ribs, and then it clumsily ran off to the bar in search of food. He watched us with a smile but didn't touch the cat.

It soon got dark and I managed to find out a few basic things about him. The name Balša means a big, strong guy. He was thirty-two and a cook at the camp. He'd recently come out of a long relationship that ended through no fault of his own. His ex-girlfriend was a Muslim and he emphasised that because he had a theory that they treat men much better than those of us who aren't. I felt a hidden need to show myself better than her, and it annoyed me that he'd introduced an obstacle into our relationship that I had to overcome.

Night drowned the day and we became impulsive. The mosquitoes were unbearable and I counted exactly thirty-one bites, but the sky was enormous and bright, and I imagined it coming down to earth and burying us. I don't

Katarina Mitrović

know why I had such thoughts, but he interrupted them by pulling on my hand – we had to 'get something done'.

We left the beach on a dirt track, and the grass turned to deep, sharp undergrowth that hid small animals. I didn't want him to see I was afraid, but I slowed down a bit because the fear was stronger than me.

'Are you chicken?'

He started to laugh, so I relaxed and quickened my pace. He took me resolutely by the arm, and I surrendered to his strong grip and warmth. There were a few more turns, in utter darkness; I stepped on some small creature, and then we finally arrived. It was a caravan in the middle of nowhere. Only a blue light bulb could be seen illuminating the interior and the faces of a few men. They were sitting with their heads half bowed. Drugs were on the table, I guessed, but I didn't look. I felt and found a swing suspended between two trees. Fear of fear. I got onto it and tried to transform it into a pleasant experience. I smacked my leg and a spot remained there. The mosquito fell to the ground.

When he was done, he groped his way to me in the dark and we went back to the beach. My friends were sleeping, each in her own tent. There was a large rotary washing hoist with clothes drying. It turned and creaked. It was covered with insects that looked as if they'd been sewn on. Next to it was a wooden stand with a mattress. We sat down on it.

He lay down, to be exact, but I sat because I felt it would be stupid for me to lie down with him straight away. I looked at the nearby hangar. That was where he slept with the other workers. I became uncomfortable in that semi-sitting position and my arm went to sleep. He brought beer from the bar, which we drank in large gulps. I was glad because alcohol relaxes me. I love a cold beer on a hot summer day. Or whiskey with ice cubes that crack in it. Mulled wine when it's snowing outside. Sweet liqueur. Strong *rakija* that stuns you, makes you laugh and embraces you. The feeling that everything will be alright. The feeling that I'll be able to do everything. Time is on my side. The whole world belongs to me and I belong to it. Alcohol is a gift to people who ...

'Want another beer? I can't drink any more, I've had enough.'

'Same here.'

'Sure? It's no trouble for me to go.'

'I really can't take any more.'

Another lie – I could have drunk at least three more bottles. Then he opened the topic of how many guys I'd been with, and I knew I'd have to lie about all kinds of things because the truth wasn't an option, not even theoretically. I don't even know how many men and women I've been with. Maybe between twenty and thirty. Relationships long and short, one-night stands, two-night stands, relationships until we get sick of each other, relationships until we meet someone else ...

'I had one serious relationship. We were best friends, and then we screwed it up and now we're nothing.'

He nodded in satisfaction.

'That's what I thought.'

He mentioned his Muslim ex again, and then he pulled me over to lie next to him. I was a little uncomfortable, and a little not. He played with my hand a little and before I could say anything he grabbed me and kissed me, and then he hugged me and I felt we'd known each other since childhood and just hadn't seen each other for a long time. But in the real world we'd known each other for exactly seven hours. I didn't know who this man was. That thought hit me all of a sudden and disturbed me. I said I had to sleep

84

Katarina Mitrović

and rushed to the tent. He was confused; I think he lay there for a while, and then he left too.

The dead air in the tent made me anxious. The tangled sheets were full of sand, and I hated to think how many insects had crawled in and were just waiting for me to fall asleep so they could crawl into my ears. My friend was fast asleep, but when I rolled over and tried to get comfortable, she managed to mumble:

'How was it?'

'I'm in love.'

'Moron.'

She laughed, hugged me with one arm and one leg, and fell asleep again. I pushed her arm off me a few moments later because it was sweaty. I peeked through the gauze of the tent and could see a spider swimming through the sand – you see it for a bit, then it sinks, and reappears in another place. At times I thought I couldn't breathe, as if I was in a grave. I kept waking up with a jolt all night, and I felt I could hear the distant meowing of a cat.

The next day he asked for time off but didn't get it, so I waited for him to finish his shift, which was about five in the afternoon. We walked on the beach until we were exhausted, then came back and ate the leftovers from lunch. I don't think he liked it that I drank, so I didn't insist, but he brought a bottle of wine and we went to our mattress in front of the hangar. I noticed that he drank one glass the whole time and was sober, while he kept refilling my glass. Never mind. We talked about relationships again, and then about how to raise children. Basically I got really drunk and soon we started making out. The lights in my friends' tents were off. He slipped in his hand, which was a little cold but pleasant. He was very quick and I didn't even notice him unfasten my bra. He panted deeply before he entered me. I didn't even manage to ask him about a condom. It seemed a bit stupid to me because he'd kept emphasising that one should live in the moment. He came and came inside me, and then we fell asleep on the mattress. I felt strange, and I dreamed of a tree growing in my belly and of it bursting when the branches pierced the skin.

Several hours passed, and then I woke up because I was thirsty. He wasn't beside me. My feet sank into the sand and I headed for the tap in front of the hangar. I went up to it, bent down and drank the water straight from the gush. From that perspective, I saw a pair of cat's eyes glowing in the dark. I was barefoot and silent. He was sitting on the sand with his legs spread. His bony hands were holding the cat I'd been playing with that day. Its neck was in the circle made by his fingers. He squeezed, first gently, then harder. The cat was small and weak, but it struggled and scratched him. Something in my belly started to stab me – maybe those branches. He dropped the soft body, which fell dully to the sand. He turned and looked at me.

Andrea Popov-Miletić

YOUNG PIONEERS, WE ARE SEAWEED*
(excerpt)

You wrote a story about a man who won by giving up. He could no longer piss against the wind, so he withdrew down to the Danube and befriended a carp. You called it *The Dictionary of the River*.

A few definitions from *The Dictionary of the River*:

T
Terrace – the most important place by the river, where everything happens

D
Difficult decisions – baked fish or fish stew; beer or spritzer

---

* The title is a spoof on the anthem of the socialist children's movement in Yugoslavia, whose first line went: 'O, Young Pioneers, we are the army of the truth! Every day we grow like the green grass' (Pioniri maleni, mi smo vojska prava, svakog dana rastemo k'o zelena trava). The reference to seaweed expresses the protagonist's longing for the Adriatic, which became virtually impossible for ordinary Serbian citizens to travel to after the collapse of Yugoslavia.

N
Neighbour

When he was made to retire, he bought bees
When his hives were stolen, he died
After all, he'd been a headmaster all his life

*

You didn't find a carp to commune with, but one day a creature appeared that sniffed and embraced you. It belonged to the Brotherhood of Yellow Dogs. It was a relative of all those stray yellow dogs with a black muzzle and two kindly black eyes like buttons. From that day on, you started to notice them everywhere, those duplicates, that multiplication, that kinship.

You're ten years old and not allowed to have a dog. You watch the little fish with their string-like poos, creatures that always come in pairs, that feed on small, pungent, multi-coloured nibbles. You lean a poster of Leonardo DiCaprio, a page from *SuperTeen* magazine with actors from the *Naughty Years* series up against the glass of the aquarium along with your travel pass. You find the fish dead on the spot, one after another. You stick your fingers in the water in the hope of getting a piscine kiss on the pad of a finger, and soon afterwards another of the fish would die. A new partner would soon be bought for the one that was left alone – it was impossible to tell which was the old and which the new one because they didn't differ in any way.

You've come to terms with the fact that you won't find a great love in this life, nor earn big money nor write a

Andrea Popov-Miletić

great story. What kind of story do you want anyway? You're not consistent or disciplined, you're too unruly to write anything coherent. Fragments and impressions are all that come out. You're unable to pick yourself up and get in shape. You write dialogues as if you've never spoken to another human being.

The feeling of the sea in everyday life – is there any such course, any such hypnosis? It's not about going to the sea but rediscovering the feeling you had back then, relocating the sea in yourself and around you; it's about your life being like at sea, and in the sea. A yellow typewriter stood on a desk without a chair. It would tell you: 'Stop writing about me.' It would tell you that you've written enough about Mother and death. They say you're only allowed to write a book about your childhood once. Maybe it would say: 'Stop your pouting and the me-me-me. Look around a bit, fold up the rearview mirror, look out the window and not just in the mirror.'

My mother tried to get rid of her migraines by drinking water, drinking coffee, rubbing lemon on her temples, and lying in the dark. She drank teas and medicines, went to acupuncture, a monastery and Greece, visited a bioenergetic healer and then a Herzegovinian herbalist with an overly male name, and sniffed lemon. A nascent manuscript 'in progress'. Will it ever get beyond that stage? Young, un-established writers – death will affirm you! You feel your heart and your head. Words are interchangeable little fish. We are all interchangeable little fish. You overturned the table and shouted: 'Enough!'

[...]

The swollen Danube flowed, bearing various objects: a brownish, plastic two-litre beer bottle, a pink shampoo container, plastic bags in blue, yellow and red, and then red, blue and white. A chequered couch sailed by in the middle of the riverine living room.

A dog barked all day and all night; it was something deeper than the antagonism towards cats, than the threat of the emaciated creatures by the eerie name of *jackals*, than unknown, creeping legs and hypnotising wheels. It would go down to the river for a drink of water and would stay there as if a strange restlessness had entered it, a marooned sea spirit; it would skulk along the bank, back and forth, and howl. You sometimes sing or chatter all day yourself. But this barking was different. There was nothing alive in the area except for some hazy but cheerful figures in a boat in the distance. You went down to the river, and at the GPS coordinates 45.283641°N 19.272453°E your papers were floating in the water, the manuscript you cast into the inspection pit on Mount Letenka.

A spring day, and the yellow dogs fan out and fuse together without our help – lick-lick, sniff-sniff – without the slightest inhibition. We can just be involved with naming the puppies. You only go shopping after dark when everything is less obtuse and the act more cinematic. And, lo and behold, along the road to the supermarket is a double file of black. Faces peer out of protective suits. Shields, body armour, stacked dominoes. 'Excuse me, what's going on?' you ask. 'We're here to prevent unrest.' Emotional Security* graffiti comes to mind. The guy you drank with, the one you're reading, materialised just as you were repeating the code for ox-heart tomato to yourself. You lay your heart on

* A rock band from Novi Sad.

Andrea Popov-Miletić

the scales, it's heavy, and answer awkwardly. You punch in the code and run to Frozen Vegetables. *Ankica, please go to Frozen Vegetables. Ankica, please mop the floor at Frozen Vegetables. Thanks, Ankica.* You say to yourself: 'Take the cheese, and I'll stand in line for the meat. My back hurts, so when we get home I need you to give me a massage.' In your mind you vilify him, paint him as unreliable and a loser, with a beard like a bandit, and if he cared about you he'd never let you go. 'So why are you just standing there? Why aren't you preventing unrest?'

Milica Rašić

SMELL

I named her Ina.

My mother's name was Alma. Mine is Almina. And hers – Ina.

When I arrange our names like that, they sound funny. Like a tongue-twister. Alma Almina Ina, *almaalminaina almaalminaina*. An awkward attempt to patch up life with a name.

Ina never met Alma. Alma, my mother, died when we were being driven to the border. I remember two soldiers propping her up, since she could hardly stand in the jam-packed military vehicle. There were too many of those muddy people and a few less muddy soldiers. The soldiers were gambling with death by transporting us unknown wretches to the border. They looked as if they weren't doing what they were doing, with their eyes fixed above our heads and slightly askew so they'd see neither us nor themselves. It was as if they were deleting us with their gaze, killing the time with which they were prolonging our lives. To the border. There we would be handed over to others.

Alma, my mother, simply expired. It was as if she was tired of everything. I couldn't blame her. Her head drooped onto the shoulder of the soldier who was holding her firmly by the arm. His eyes had been at half-mast for a while already. It looked as if both of them fell asleep standing up.

I told them to take her out and leave her by a tree as soon as we turned off the road and got closer to the forest. They looked at me as if I was speaking a foreign language.

'But she's your ...'

'Yes, she's my mother. But she's dead. I can't carry her with me, and she's a burden to you. You could get killed out here.'

Mute and tired, they still just stared at me.

'Don't get killed because of a woman who's dead. Chuck her out.'

It's Alma's fault I'm like that. *Unscrupulously rational*, she used to say. *You have to be unscrupulously rational if you want to survive.* Then I did what my dead mother said, and the soldiers obeyed. As soon as we left the road, we stopped, turned off the headlights, waited several minutes to make sure no one was following us, and then they opened the door.

'Wait!' I yelled.

I went up to her, tore the collar off her dirty white shirt and put it in my pocket.

'OK,' I said and turned my back.

I didn't raise Alma's collar to my nose for a long time. I didn't even cry. I saved my tears for better times.

I didn't look when they took her out. I think they were gentle because I didn't hear the body hit the ground. Only soldiers like that could be traitors, I thought. They were much too considerate. Although it was impossible, I could already smell the decay that would soon consume Alma's body. And that is still the undying image of my mother – that body lying at the edge of the forest in the rain; and it's still the face of an old and once beautiful woman. But that face was now just a mask, and her body a pile of bones and flesh that the rain was helping fast become food for the earth. *Whose piece of earth?* I wondered at the time.

*

Almaalminaina. Sometimes that tongue-twister comes to me out of the blue when I'm hanging up the washing or cooking dinner.

It had been a long time since Ina, my daughter, asked me about the war.

She came home from school one day waving some paper and smiling from ear to ear.

'Look, Mum! I've won a prize!'

'Really? What for?'

Without a word, she handed me her prize and shut herself away in her room.

It was a story. Her story. Mine, actually. About the war we emerged from *as victors*, as she put it: she, yet unborn, and I, who lost my mother along the way. She wrote about an experience she never had but constructed – as I concluded – on the basis of stories she'd googled. It reminded me of Alma. Shutting herself away and ruminating.

I went into her room and threw what she'd written onto the bed.

'You have no idea about the war.'

She was silent, with a pre-emptively downcast look.

'But the story is beautiful.'

For Ina, war is something far away, something you read about while drinking cocoa and eating dates. For me, war is a dull, tearing pain in the groin: when you're defiantly silent but there's no place for your defiance in that cramped world; when you don't know if you're already dead because you don't feel this kind of thing when you're alive; you say a silent prayer that it will be over quickly and there won't be much blood; when you imagine spitting in the faces of all four of them at the end. But, when you manage to stand up again, slowly, because you can barely feel your legs, they're already gone.

Ina never asked me who her father was. *Don't ask questions you know have no answers*, my mother, Alma used to say. I don't know how, but Ina knew that.

Alma's white collar didn't smell of decay. When I realised that, when I finally raised it to my nose, I cried like rain. The rain that soaked Alma's body in the forest. I hope they laid her on her back, facing the sky. *At least there was no funeral*, the thought went through my mind every time I imagined her lifeless face on the ground. The war was a good excuse, so maybe not completely without benefit. I hate funerals. *A crowd of people wasting their time on someone who's no longer there*, Alma would say. Not being buried would have appealed to her. As long as they turned her to face the sky.

The collar smelled of lavender. Alma grew lavender in the courtyard and laid the drying laundry on it to absorb the scent. That made our courtyard a shambles, as if dogs had cast up clothes on the bushes, but in return we always smelled of lavender. It was an unforgettable scent. Pure, untainted. *One scent*, Alma would say. She didn't like perfumes because *they put all kinds of gunk in them*. But: *lavender is lavender*.

How is it possible that someone is gone but their smell remains? Memories are nothing compared to smell. Memories mellow as time passes. Smell is relentless – the living breath of a body that's no longer alive.

I inhaled the scent of lavender from Alma's collar for months until it evaporated.

*

Ina still didn't ask me about the war. And then she decided to study international relations. She received a scholarship to study abroad and was preparing to leave. Although I didn't ask her, I knew why she wanted to go to Bosnia in particular. The more I kept silent about the war, the more strongly she wanted to study it – in the very country where it happened. *Again, you won't learn anything about it, my child*, I told her inside. *You'll never know the smell of war.* That's why I let her go.

The evening before the trip, she went into my room and opened the wardrobe. *I want to take something of yours with me*, she said. I had no idea what she'd do with my things when she had too many of her own; she reluctantly left some because there was no more room in her suitcase. I wandered around the house and pretended to be doing something, as if it were a day like any other. I didn't want her to sense the tears ready to flow at any moment if only I stopped.

Alma, my mother, was constantly wandering about the house. Her steps were like continuous music, like the rattle of a train. The sound of her steps was proof to me that time didn't stand still. Maybe Ina heard my steps in the same way. When she goes there, she won't hear them any more.

Milica Rašić

'What is THIS?' she shouted from the depths of the wardrobe. I went into my room, and Ina was sitting among my scattered things and holding Alma's collar.

'What is it, Mum? It smells of lavender.'

Almaalminaina almaalminaina. I cried like the rain.

Published with the kind permission of Biber,
a short story contest for socially engaged short
stories in Albanian, BCMS and Macedonian.
The Biber team is part of the Centre
for Nonviolent Action – Sarajevo/Belgrade.

Milica Rašić

Svetlana Slapšak

I'M WRITING
TO YOU
FROM BELGRADE

It was dark and would be for a long time. Only her study existed, in bright colours, with discreet light bulbs in the shelves to illuminate her books, with a huge, free-standing desk from wall to wall, and warmth coming from the floor, under the window and everywhere. Schliemann and Dinah liked her room the most and chose the part of the desk near the window for their daytime naps that lasted hours. At night, they left her alone and snuck into bed with Goran or Julka. After all, she didn't sleep well given the small differences between day and night here, so she often made up for it during the day by dozing in the armchair with the cats. Schliemann had only recently begun showing that he was older than Dinah: his fur had become bristly and was thinning a bit, and when she stroked his back she could count all the protruding vertebrae, although he wasn't thin. His gaze was still wild and bright, his voice still fierce and funny when he opened his disproportionately large jaws, but there was weariness in his body. Now Schliemann mostly slept, only waking up when Milica entered the room, and then he'd accompany things with a heavy, deeply emotional meow. Dinah, curled up next to him, kept her old shape, but pain could be seen in her eyes: she'd had three tumour operations and the vet thought she shouldn't be operated on again. Her soft white belly, normally covered in long hair, had only just healed and the last scar was still visible in the short, spiky fur.

'Getting old, Schliemann, eh?' Milica spoke to them her usual way.

Schliemann deigned to half open his eyes and send her a sharp, thin beam of light from the shadow between the grey sky and the screen of her computer. The flat was on the seventh floor, and a little fog, rain or snow made it impossible to see anything outside except the distant lights of downtown Toronto.

'You've never made prophecies …'

Schliemann lowered his head onto his front paws but kept looking at her.

'I won't bother you with my usual cosmic associations when I look at you.'

Schliemann closed his eyes, stretched his paws and showed his claws – a sign that he still felt like dozing.

She caressed him behind the ears and on his back. Schliemann made a barely audible moan of pleasure and turned his head so he could stroke his chin.

'Not the look that would explain the meaning of life to me,' Milica mused.

She continued to pet him. Unlike Dinah, who would have scratched her at the first sign of slackening attention and dedication, Schliemann was satisfied with less and gratefully began to purr, first grating and ragged, then more evenly. Milica clicked on her translation file with her right hand and caressed Schliemann with the left.

At that moment, Goran's voice came from the other room – first he whistled as usual, and then shouted:

'Come here, you won't believe it!'

She got up with a sigh.

'I hope you've called me for a good reason ...'

'Slobodan Milošević died last night,' Goran said, standing in front of the television. 'I don't feel anything. No relief, no fear, nothing at all.'

'There will be no relief,' Milica said. 'But I'm afraid there will be fear because he died without being brought to justice ...'

'What difference does it make to us?' Goran said after a brief silence. 'The country we once lived in no longer exists. We have to tend our memories so they don't disappear in a puff of smoke, and that's very hard here. Do you sometimes feel we've sailed to a distant shore, from which there's no return?'

'Nothing is certain. What if Julka decides to explore what remains of her parents' world?'

'At least I can be sure about you,' Goran smiled. 'Where the cats are, I'll always find you.'

She heard herself ask the awkward and rather stupid question: 'Why?'

'Because of Julka,' he replied with his head bowed, but firmly. 'And when we get old – really old – I hope you'll accept me like another geriatric cat, however your life may be.'

'Why are you always sure it's you who'll need care, not me?' but she couldn't hide her smile.

'Do you want me to crack open a bottle? Champagne, or we've got another St Emilion ...'

'The latter,' she said. 'I'll bring some cheese and olives.'

The snow stopped falling. A clear silver line appeared in the middle of the sky – a sign that a new front was coming. They sipped their wine without a word by the screen with the sound turned off.

Svetlana Slapšak

That's how Julka found them when she came back from school. They didn't hear her, nor did she announce that she was back. She took off her heavy boots and polar jacket in the hall, peeked into Milica's room to check where Schliemann and Dinah were, then slipped silently into her own room. Her tall, powerful body, no longer childlike, with a magnificent broad brow, had little space in the small bedroom. But Julka's mini-kingdom suited her perfectly as long as no one but the cats came in.

Milica heard a sound and turned her head.

'It's OK, I'll go,' Goran said as he got up and headed for the kitchen. She remained, glass in hand, her legs up on a stool and her head cast back. She felt that time, as well as Julka, Goran and the cats, who were slowly heading for the kitchen, had passed her by and she remained on her little snow cloud, lost in oblivion, strangely calm, expecting death or a louder sound. After what seemed like a century, the latter came: Goran called out that it was dinner time.

That's how she used to return to her mother's kitchen after crying, arguing with Dara or making love to Slobo: with an indeterminable sense of guilt, surprised that that form of existence still existed. And it did: in Julka's radical youthful disengagement from the world, in Goran's rock-solid belief in their lifelong union, and in the aged cats that rubbed up affectionately against her legs.

'I've just reheated the soup from lunch and added some chicken to the salad. Will that be enough for you?'

'More than enough,' Julka replied. 'I'm going to make myself carrot and lemon juice. Anyone else want some?'

'No, dear. We oldies are allowed to have something stronger today,' Goran said.

'Because Slobo kicked the bucket? No one at school was interested today. Come on, Goran, enlighten me a bit. We can also turn on the French current-affairs programme – maybe they'll have something more to say about it.'

'My teenage Valkyrie,' Goran smiled.

'Mum needs time to herself. Maybe she'll even feel sorry for him,' Julka said.

Milica shook her head: she'd been so afraid for her child in the new world, where school was dumber and students less predictable, and where she had to consider carefully what to say to the teacher. But instead of drowning in trauma, her miraculous daughter had developed a cold rationality that allowed her to cope perfectly, effortlessly. She chose and managed her passions by herself, didn't pine for anything, and, although still half-child, developed a self-confidence far beyond her mother's and father's.

She left father and daughter in lively conversation and checked her emails. Slobo wrote to tell her about the death of his namesake and mentioned that he'd be passing through Toronto again the following month. When would Dara call?

*

Dear Milica, I couldn't have chosen a worse time for going to Belgrade. Or I chose it subconsciously – it wouldn't have been the first time! I arrived the day Slobo died. And I had to stay a few more days on business, until his funeral.

But I'll start from the beginning of the terrible trip. I had to go to Zagreb first, which has turned grey and yellow, and the city is full of small, unsightly bars. I looked for a long time to find a decent second-hand bookshop. I had to stay two days longer because Sarajevo was fogbound and it was impossible to fly. Then, in the snow and sleet of Sarajevo, I wanted to put on blinkers like a draught horse to shut out the misery. Impossible.

There are too many pockmarked and dilapidated buildings,
white cemeteries climbing the hill at the end of every street ...
and then you see insane glass cubes with advertisements. Who
shops in those malls? Most people look poor. I retreated to my
hotel room with red wine as soon as I finished work: if I opened
the window the fog would push its way in with the smell of burek
and meat on the spit, voices and wailing music ... how can these
people listen to Serbian turbo-folk after all that's happened?
On the third evening, the phone rang: Zorica. I wouldn't have
been able to find her otherwise. Zorica is shrunken and drawn –
half the woman she used to be. She lost all the fingers on her
left hand, but she copes and can even light a cigarette by herself.
She lives on a war-veteran's pension and doesn't complain. We
talked late into the night about everything except the two most
important things: Šemsa and Dušan. Then she invited me to her
place. She lives far from the centre, in a small flat in a high-rise
building. The smells are indescribable, the plaster is peeling and
the neon lights flicker and murmur. Then you enter her flat and
it's a different world. How she's arranged those thirty square
metres of hers! Everything is in discreet warm tones. Only the
most essential furniture, but comfortable. The kitchen is all in
white embroidery, decorative plants and spices on the window.
Her miniature studio is on the glazed balcony. There she paints
portraits of Šemsa – her sole motif. The flat's full of them, and
she's good at it! She took out a bottle of herb brandy, put it on a
doily, and took out two more for the glasses. We put our feet up
on the low table so the real conversation could begin.

She told me that, after Šemsa's disappearance, she became
religious. 'Which faith?' I asked stupidly. 'Hers,' she answered.
'So I made my way to Bosnia, crossing the lines of all the ar-
mies, arrived in Sarajevo and became a fighter. I no longer did
anything without asking her. I called on her every time I was
down, and she always answered. When the shrapnel took off my

fingers, she sat on my bed while the shooting went on outside. She was there to close my eyes before every operation.' 'How many times?' I asked. 'Five, I think' Zorica said. After the war, she found Šemsa's parents' house in Višegrad. They were killed with the group that was burnt – some dead, some still alive – in that big house by the river. Thanks to her position, she was able to have the house repaired and restored, and in the end, it was given to her because there was no one left of the family. She handed the house over to a young couple without any recompense as long as they didn't remove the memorial plaque for Šemsa that she'd put up on the wall near the door. 'I go there to check every now and again. I know exactly where Šemsa is,' she finally said around three in the morning. 'She went to Lake Perućac. The bodies of those who were killed in Višegrad – her whole family – and people from smaller towns all ended up there, downriver. Everyone knows about the bodies in the reservoir that cannot go anywhere. To find them, the water needs to be drained. And it will be done. I'll be there when it is, and I'll find her. She drowned herself there. Do you think she couldn't stand it anymore?'

I didn't know what to say. Šemsa had never been a coward. We told ourselves that over and over again, heaping more and more burdens and responsibilities on ourselves to try and relieve the burden for the other. After a litre of herb brandy, all we could do was cry. I woke up on the couch, wrapped in a blanket, and Zorica wasn't home. She came back around noon; she'd obviously got up early. She was visiting 'her people', as she calls them – several penniless old women and a few more 'cases' (an old expression of hers again), mostly raped and abandoned women, who no one wants to hear of any more, and who have to undergo an ordeal to get a pension. She looked as if she just got out of a rose-petal bath.

In short, to round things off: Zorica is indestructible. I had to leave the hotel and move in with her so we could talk. On the

Svetlana Slapšak

day of my departure, fog fell again: Zorica called one of those in eternal debt to her, who was to drive me to Belgrade. Parting with her was simple, without further ado. We're sure to see each other again – she's an invaluable source for the many things I still hope to get off the ground. 'She saved my life,' the driver said laconically as soon as I'd settled in my seat. He smoked in silence for the rest of the trip. We passed through a wasteland dotted with improvisations. The highlight was Arizona, a rough-and-ready centre for buying, bartering and selling, a whole city of billboards and covered stalls. At the border, where we had to wait three hours, I tried to pay the driver but he refused each time. All he'd accept was a carton of cigarettes I bought in no-man's-land.

I had a lot to do in Belgrade: I gave the studio to Sava and Kreba, who came out as a queer couple – better late than never – and were consequently kicked out of their homes by their parents and most of their friends. Both are unemployed: Sava sells software, while Kreba repairs computers and games: no one cares about trademarks and copyrights here. Then I had to wrest Dušan's flat out of his family's hands once more, and now another human-rights initiative is moving in. Well, at least I chose them myself. They don't pay rent, but the flat remains mine in case they screw things up badly.

Belgrade, my dear, has narrowed: parked cars block the streets and alleys, and the balconies of indescribably ugly and aggressive new buildings collide overhead. Former Revolution Boulevard is constricted, not only by all the kiosks and stalls but also by those alien buildings whose mirrored glass windows, plaster lions and eagle-topped fences intrude into your field of vision. The most common kind of shop is a bakery: people still have money for that.

I went to Dušan's grave at the New Cemetery: what a struggle it was to get a casket for his ashes. Mladenka's grave had been tidied and there were fresh flowers. The main paths have been narrowed to make another row of graves. Business thrives at the cemetery; new names are carved into gravestones that obviously originate from the century before last, and some of the dilapidated angels in the elite section near the entrance have been replaced by 'modern' tombstones with portraits of hipsters and gangsters.

I'm sitting in bed in a brand-new 'boutique' hotel, and everything's OK except that I don't know how to sit on the chair, which is a most unusual shape. The TV is on, with the sound turned down, and I see a pageant of boobs and arses, and the occasional butcher's apprentice. An advertisement appears for a few seconds in the corner of the window with a fanciful coat of arms: it's the latest fashion to trace a business back to at least the 1870s, when the great-great-great-grandfather of the new capitalist supposedly established the family firm. I have bills to pay when I get back, so I'm going through them.

Sorry I'm so tired and cynical. I thought I'd mastered Belgrade and our former world, that I'd abandoned that compulsive anthropology akin to dissection, and then I realised I haven't. I'm just waiting for you to snap and go on holiday to Dubrovnik and Belgrade instead of the Dominican Republic. I wish I could tell you that we and the troubles of our time are past and gone, but they're not. Memory is irrevocably marked by hatred. And I'd thought that maybe not everything was weak, and that there were other things and values worth upholding ...

The main thing I actually want to tell you is that, since I hadn't been watching the news, I didn't realise that Slobo was being brought back for his funeral: first to Belgrade and then to his home town.* I'd been to see another lawyer, in an unimaginably luxurious office at the beginning of Crnogorska Street,

---

* Former Yugoslav and Serbian leader Slobodan Milošević died in custody in The Hague, in 2006.

Svetlana Slapšak

and then took a taxi. It was raining – the kind of rain that comes from everywhere and nowhere. At the second traffic light in Gavrilo Princip Street, near the Faculty of Economics, the taxi driver had to stop. An endless river of people, Slobo's supporters, was crossing the intersection, coming from the bus station. These were his most faithful minions: not farmers or youth, but simple folk from deep, small-town Serbia – places where army coffins were sent, but not money, and no one cared or helped. They were mostly elderly, and many were cripples. A funeral audience, you might say, but they didn't even have Sunday best to wear to a funeral. Did they come because they got a meal on the way? Most likely. They were dressed in whatever they had, and it wasn't much: a tattered sheepskin coat over a summer dress, tracksuits paired with jumpers, tight coats over jeans, leather jackets over baggy flannel pants. The shoes were the worst – worn, warped and scuffed. Shoes are expensive and always wear out. Bodies that didn't fit the clothes any more – too big or too small. Wet scarves and half-dyed hair. They smoked as they walked, and their walk was slow and tired, all in the same direction, up the steps to the Green Wreath neighbourhood. The taxi driver switched on the wipers and took a cigarette. We waited almost half an hour at that traffic light, and the cars didn't dare to start even when the lights were green. We went fifty or sixty metres to the next traffic light, and there was an even bigger river of people wanting to go via Balkanska Street to Terazije. I watched them again, and the composition was the same. They didn't talk to each other, perhaps because they were afraid, but neither were they wearing a funeral expression. They'd come to speak their mind in the city they hated, after having had a bit to eat and maybe to drink. I saw it in the way they glowered at the people in the cars and those who weren't with them in the column. But most terrifying of all was the way they stared in the windows of food shops, kiosks and cafes: they were structurally hungry. We waited at the traffic lights for about forty minutes and then made our way through at a spot where the procession had thinned a bit. The taxi driver said nothing and just sighed audibly. He charged me the anticipated amount, taking no account of the taximeter.

What brought them to Belgrade apart from the free ride, sandwiches and yoghurt? That was enough. But there must have been something else. Perhaps the memory of an era when, mostly full and satisfied, they went out of their furnished flats and took to the streets because they'd been bombarded with the idea that they were being robbed? Or was it the power they felt for the first time after so many years of dormancy? The freedom to kill others who irritated them by being so incredibly similar? The post-Yugoslav freedoms were a blow to them, nothing positive. Now they'd come to bury their memory but not the belief that, as soon as a new benefactor came along who dealt liberally in other people's deaths, they could punish the first person the ray of their frustration fell on. Until then, those who still had the strength would beat and thrash whoever they got their hands on at home, as well as out and about, whenever they felt the need. What about those who wept in fear at the first free elections? I still remember them, mostly women. With no support, that part was condemned to freeze and starve in unheated studio flats or out on the street, to fish for food in rubbish bins – ten years after the war's end! They're not surrounded by the ruined houses of the neighbours they killed and they can't vent their frustration every time they go by. But now they pass by the enormous, extended cemeteries of Serbs killed on distant fronts in the First World War. All their churches, bars and party offices are full of infamous thieves and murderers who've long boasted of their deeds; their eyes are full of the repulsive plastic bodies they cultivate their unfulfilled desire on, and women are taught to become the same – pitiable dolls with frozen brains. Every letter, word or sentence around them, spoken or written (if they're still literate), teaches them hatred, envy and hopelessness. What else could they be ready for other than a new war? And if someone comes along and decides to prime them for that …

But I'd rather tell you about something else. Your mother – in case her reports don't tell you the truth – has real staying power: she's taken in a bearded, taciturn old man, an international-relations journalist who was kicked out of his job and then out of his flat shortly before retirement. He stayed wherever he could for almost three years. He looks at her with love, if that's any sign for you, and has occupied your room with his maps and papers. Your mother whispered to me that he's writing a book in English. She still drafts projects for at least ten NGOs, translates manuals and sells your translations – she's very busy, as usual. A ginger tom with a spot on his eye slinks around the house together with a very elegant black-and-white cat, with a part, jabot and socks.

I'm finishing this off at the airport in Budapest. I came by minibus from Belgrade in the foulest March weather imaginable, and I've been waiting here for six hours. I'll probably have to sleep in Frankfurt. If everything goes well, I'll be home the day after tomorrow, with good, fast broadband. What are you doing for Easter?

How about going for a spin with Julka? Bo is off to some congress in Singapore and I'll be alone at home. We could have an orgy of nostalgia for Yugo times. How are things with you? Anyone in sight? A ravishing blond (they're best when they're grey) – a Canadian lumberjack? At least you could persuade Goran and Julka to come down my way. Here the snow is gone, the magnolias and the dogwood in the garden are budding, and we could go to the sea.

Have you ever thought about old age – I mean the real thing? Wouldn't it be good to plan for a few of us to shack up somewhere together, to tend our common memory when we start to go se-nile? In Serbo-Croatian?

Lena Ruth Stefanović

ZHENYA

Zhenya threw off the blanket and got up from her wooden bed at seven fifteen, like every other working day. Still half asleep, she went the five steps that separated her bed from the low table with the electric kettle. Splashing her face with cold water, brushing her teeth and putting on her face cream took three minutes; combing and plaiting her hair about five. Then she drank her tea standing, pulled on the clothes she'd put out the night before, left the flat at seven thirty and went down the steep stairs to meet another day, almost identical to the one before and the one that would follow.

The routine was punctuated here and there by unexpected events, but they were rarely pleasant. The surprises mostly went to complicate and prolong her routine, but never – so far – to interrupt or at least postpone it. The previous day, for example, the bus she used to take to work didn't come, so she walked; sometimes the light bulbs in the stairwell of her building burned out, which made it difficult to go down the steep stairs. Pleasant interruptions, on the other hand, were predictable, long-awaited and short-lived: May Day, New Year's Day, a long weekend for Victory Day or 8 March, her birthday and nameday – and that basically exhausted the list of pleasures.

'Appropriate' films were occasionally screened in the House of Culture, a concrete dinosaur that had survived the Soviet era, usually ahead of local elections, and dances were organised every first Saturday of the month. The music there was played in blocks: thirty minutes of domestic recordings, and then thirty minutes of foreign. At twenty-three, Zhenya fell into the category of being too old to hop about on the improvised dance floor with the local ginks. Moreover, according to the provincial definition of girlhood, only about two years separated her from the category of a hopeless spinster, but Zhenya didn't think about that, nor about much else; she accepted most things as givens that were not be questioned, let alone changed. Reality was as it was, the only known one, and it had to be accepted humbly and meekly; she'd learned about it at school and she heard about it in church, where she went as robotically as she did to work and to the screenings of appropriate films ahead of elections; that's what the majority did, just as their parents had done. They'd go on to raise children who would do the same – half-asleep, with forwards as the default direction and only the occasional step to the left or right conceivable, without diverging too much from the fixed trajectory and the majority of their companions, step by step, from crib to grave. Following this predictable path without excessive oscillation, tiresome thought and inappropriate questions, the statistically average resident of Ignoransk would live up to both the State's and the Church's ideal of a citizen and would exit life's stage just as quietly. Those who violated this silence in any way were considered thugs, except when they seized power, in which case they were to be considered not thugs but ideological guides and leaders. That's how it had been forever, which in Zhenya's mind encompassed the period of her mother's and grandmother's life, that is about a hundred years; whatever was before that – probably God alone knew, and it didn't concern our heroine.

There were few men, and they never stayed long; women spent their lives mostly with other women, and a typical family, like Zhenya's, consisted of a grandmother, a mother and a child. Fathers were largely away on 'business trips', often lasting decades, or drunkenly roamed the suburbs; in any case, they belonged to a very rare and fickle species; those exceptions who allowed themselves to be domesticated were most often embraced by several single-sex, three-member families at once – the male of the house would usually be considered a father, husband and son-in-law by at least two such communities, and that was alright; well, not quite alright, but certainly better than nothing at all.

Vilior, who introduced himself as Vova and concealed his real name, cursed the potholed roads and the province to which they led; the insidious blows that the broken asphalt inflicted on his newly acquired, quasi-German pride – a 2001 Audi A4 – stabbed him deep inside; he would almost have preferred to be hit in the head himself than to hear the thuds each time that queen of Bavaria went over a deep Russian pothole.

His maternal uncle, Vini, who by a strange turn of events settled in Ignoransk towards the end of his life, was seriously ill. They were informed of this by a telegram that arrived at Vilior's Moscow flat that morning. Uncle Vini had spent his entire working life as a pen-pusher in a range of extremely obscure state institutions, and, as was to be expected, became overweight and irascible; maybe he'd always been that way, Lord knows, Vilior thought as he sped to visit him.

Everyone in the family had exceedingly strange names and only used them in their full form on exceptional occasions; highly unusual names were widespread in Soviet times, and Vilior was an abbreviation of Vladimir Ilyich Lenin and the October Revolution, and it could be assumed that Vini stood for Vladimir Ilyich and ... All depending on the imagination of the godparents, or whatever the surrogates of godparents were called in those times. Uncle Vini's real name was Benjamin, but that fact was known to few beyond the inner family circle and the staff of the registration office and other relevant departments, whose job it was to establish the facts. For everyone else, that relative was Uncle (or Comrade) Vini.

Uncle or Comrade Vini ended up in out-of-the-way Ignoransk after meeting a certain young Komsomol girl on holiday in a Party sanatorium; by marrying him, she became comrade and aunt number four. Why this new aunt didn't move to Moscow to live with her aging husband, which one expected in such circumstances, was not known, but Uncle Vini's move from the capital to the backwoods presumably had something to do with his divorce from a Party central committee member's daughter, which some of those in the know called treason. In any case, the influence of Uncle Vini's ex-father-in-law meant the capital was too small for both of them, so Vini went to live with his young wife in her modest home, as unexpected as this turn of events in a summer romance was.

Events soon took an even stranger turn when the Komsomol aunt fled to the West, leaving behind her aging husband and the modest flat in the multi-storey building where Zhenya lived with her mother and grandmother. Nothing more was known about the Komsomol aunt who defected to the decadent West, and her deserted husband was eventually accepted by the tenants of the building, despite his arrogance.

One night, an exhausted Zhenya, who was returning from work at the factory, collided on the steep staircase, where the light bulb had burned out, with Vilior, affectionately called Vova, who had just arrived on the potholed road from Moscow. Thus began an unusual acquaintance.

Fashion trends, which in Moscow changed with the seasons, resisted time in Ignoransk; as in the past, women wore cotton dresses, plain on ordinary days and with a floral pattern on holidays; their uncut hair was woven into thick braids; figures were rounded and cheeks ruddy.

Vilior felt he'd landed in the middle of a filmset for a historical movie. All the props were there: Stalinist architecture, women in chintz dresses, a Youth Centre and organised dances. The only thing now missing was Stalin himself – the monument, which had once paraded the central square, was removed with zeal equal to that with which it was once erected.

It could be said that life in this small town rather amused him at first – he was well and truly sick of Moscow and the Muscovites.

Vilior had grown up on Leninsky Avenue in the capital and proudly wore that stamp, which forever separated him from the millions of ordinary people who came from less elegant neighbourhoods and less desirable circumstances. His seemingly careless way of dressing set him apart from the crowd, which was still trying hard to look classy, new and rich. Even his pronunciation – the way he arrogantly broke off and shortened drawn-out Russian vowels – automatically placed him in the urban caste, which is aloof and unattainable unless you've had the good fortune of being born into it. He was educated here and there: several diplomas from prestigious Moscow educational institutions, acquired partly through his parents' connections and partly through their money, lay neatly piled on his desk with no prospect of being used for the purpose they were issued for; after all, a successful man in our century is not even expected to be overly smart.

Moscow, Vova's Moscow, was a world unto itself – an oasis of the advantaged, a precinct of the privileged, a time capsule of the chosen. Ignoransk belonged to the others, the supernumeraries, who had no place in elite Moscow. Vova rarely went beyond the famous MKAD, the ring road that separated Moscow from the rest of Russia and people like him from others – the disadvantaged, underprivileged and unchosen. The latter considered the inhabitants of the capital indulgent snobs; for Muscovites, they were a rabble driven by herd instincts, not much different to cattle.

The night when Vova, tired from the journey, collided with Zhenya on the dark staircase, he still considered his stay in the province an unnecessary deviation from his urbanite orbit, which may have bored him but was the only one worth living for, and he felt this deviation to be like the Era of Stagnation, painful precisely because of its inevitability.

He attached no importance to the unexpected encounter on the stairs. After colliding with the neighbour, he apologised for his carelessness, wished her a good evening and introduced himself; in Moscow he wouldn't have bothered – people crash into each other all the time and pay no heed because they'll probably never meet again – but in Ignoransk everything was different.

It was dark on the staircase and Zhenya couldn't see the new tenant very well, but she was excited by the encounter – the timbre of his voice, his speech and his smell made her return to her flat on the wings of a strange new feeling. She took her coat off in the hall and went into the kitchen, the family headquarters where the three women gathered. Her mother and grandmother noticed something resembling a smile on Zhenya's face and were greatly surprised; people rarely smiled in that town unless they had very good reason to.

'What happened?' her mother asked in a whisper.

'Nothing,' Zhenya answered after a short silence.

Her mother said nothing more. She looked at her own mother and the two women tacitly agreed, with their eyes, that some event had brought that smile to Zhenya's face.

Meanwhile, in the flat opposite, Vova was unpacking, accompanied by his uncle's grumbling. The old man moaned almost constantly, rarely for any good reason, and this had almost become the most recognisable feature of his character. He was usually dissatisfied with the atmospheric conditions and the state of society, and especially with everyday life and the surroundings in which he lived. But if we ignore this trait of his, he was in fact a perfectly decent old chap, firmly convinced that the world was on the highway to hell. The Russian idea, the meaning of history and the providential role of Russia in its dramatic course, as well as other 'accursed questions', had ultimately bored him; besides, how much time can an intelligent person devote to thinking about the mission of their nation when they have no influence over it? He resolved that maybe there was still hope for the youngest and least corrupted, so he read the pedagogical literature of Anton Makarenko, who was in vogue again, and also of Abraham Flexner, who was no longer banned.

Inspired by his nephew's presence during the long winter evenings, Uncle Vini lamented in his monologues, which Vova pretended to follow attentively, that pragmatism crushed inquisitiveness and that the great usefulness of the useless was almost completely ignored.

Like Nabokov's hero, Vova had grown up with the fantastic privileges of the (red) bourgeoisie, 'between a cathedral-like sideboard and the backs of dormant books.'*

Once upon a time, before the internet, Vova read. He was still immune to the immoral charms of the metropolis where he was born, still an early riser and still free of harmful habits. He loved strange writers: Daniil Kharms, whose absurd stories shyly began to appear in bookshops in the early nineties; Nabokov and his meticulous style; and especially Chinghiz Aitmatov. Vova was lashed by winds from the steppes and frightened by summer storms with cloud-rending thunder as he devoured the tale of love for national culture and the Soviet machine that came packaged in the legend of the aging bard Raimaly-aga's love for the young Begima; it was also contained in the accounts about Yedigei's tribe, and in the story of Jamila, who carries sacks of grain to the railway station in the company of a wounded newcomer to the village, while her husband is away on the battlefield, possessing everything she needs ... until wounded Daniyar sings. In reality, Soviet management of Central Asia was difficult and even more problematic than the Tsarist order that preceded it; nomadic cultures with their centuries-old systems had to enter into a marriage of convenience with the highly centralised communist bureaucracy, for which they'd only ever be remote provinces on the fringe of a powerful empire in modern times, since the conquests of Alexander the Great have become ancient history and the Silk Road is irrelevant.

Vova stopped reading books when first Moscow, and then all of Russia, consigned the classics to the shelves and

---

* Vladimir Nabokov: *The Gift*. Translated from the Russian by Michael Scammel in collaboration with the author. Vintage International, New York, 1963. p. 43.

turned on the TV, which, ironically, broadcast the reality show Big Brother. Most reality-TV viewers knew nothing about Aitmatov, nor about Orwell and the prototype Big Brother, and the rest of the world could breathe a sigh of relief because now this nation, too, fell to commercialism and its companion – apathy.

In Ignoransk, where time stood still, Vova found Zhenya interesting in a rather bizarre way. It amused him to listen to her thoughts made up of stereotypes, her judgements, which were commonplaces, the folk sayings she used, along with banal comparisons and archaic adjectives that had long since fallen out of use in Moscow. Never before had he spent so much time with a person who seemed to be of a dying species spawned by Soviet morality, glorification of the proletariat and faith in the bright future of communism.

There had been no specimens of Zhenya's kind in the cities for a long time – only in the provinces, which didn't speak foreign languages, travel or use the internet, could people like her be found.

Vova brought turmoil to Zhenya's previously predictable life, and she began to follow that feeling, accompanying it further and further after the events that ensued – even to Moscow.

Uncle Vini's condition worsened again and Vova extended his stay in Ignoransk until the end of March, when a first-year student and rapper, who went by the unusual name of Lensky, arrived from St Petersburg on holiday in the building where Zhenya and Uncle Vini lived. Lensky's grandmother lived on the ground floor of the building, and in the flat opposite there was an absent-minded teacher and his wife, an employee of the district administration. Lensky was in love with their daughter, Olya.

There are no secrets in Ignoransk, and Vova was soon introduced to Lensky's love story. Because of Olya, he spent every semester break at his grandmother's. Idleness and general lethargy saw Vova become friends with the much younger Lensky, whose rhymes and infatuation with Olya made him laugh.

Muscovites would call Olya a bimbette; in Ignoransk they called her a coquette and cock-teaser. Before a series of circumstances (Zhenya's birthday, a dinner party with the neighbours and a drunken flirt) led to a fight between Vova and Lensky over Olya, before the rapper ended up in casualty with a skull fracture and Vova realised it was time to return to the city – before all those events, Zhenya declared her love for Vova. Vova was taken aback, rejected Zhenya's love and finally travelled home to Moscow.

Driven by restlessness, Zhenya, too, was soon on her way to Moscow.

I wonder what to do with my Zhenya. If I borrowed and followed Pushkin's plot, she'd move to Moscow (the court no longer being in St Petersburg), marry an oligarch close to the president with a capital P and become one of the famous women from Rublyovka, the richest village in the world, where the Russian *nouveaux riches* live; Vova would meet her again three years later and go crazy for her. She'd still be in love with him but, being wed to another, would remain faithful to her husband, and inconsolable Vova would go off to wander Southeast Asia, or something like that.

But I wonder if I could contrive a more appealing and joyful future for my borrowed heroine?

Moving to Moscow was inevitable, as was losing weight and cutting off her plaits, and neither Zhenya's plaintive looks nor the pleas of conservative readers would sway me.

Zhenya could work on personal change, achieve enlightenment and become a spiritual teacher; she could travel to India or Tibet, and Vova would accompany her on her worldly and astral journeys. Such an ending to the story would be filled with descriptions of third-world countries, where people should be poor, but spiritual and happy, and this would be a serious rebuke to the decadent West and Westernised Russia. Zhenya would become aware of the archetypes from the collective subconscious that trained her to think and speak as before; she'd become a free human being no longer tamed by genetically conditioned modes of thought, no longer restrained by the verbal corset that transmits that thinking from one generation to another.

She'd devote the second half of her life to linguistics and designing a new language, a kind of new age Esperanto free of stereotypes and connotations, which would name objects and concepts without judging as to their essence. But I'll leave such unlikely transformations to those who imitate Dostoevsky and believe that a harlot and a murderer can awaken in Orthodoxy with tears of joy in their eyes; I'll come up with something better for my heroes.

First, I'll send them to my motherland, Montenegro, to warm up after the Russian winter. I'll ask my parents to welcome Zhenya and Vova and to treat them as guests in our hearty, homely way.

Then I'll send them on an excursion to Bari to pay homage to the relics of St Nicholas, and maybe I'll go along myself.

Zhenya will definitely begin writing – poetry, essays and meta-novels with nonlinear narratives, in which she'll acquaint my Montenegrins with the secrets of the Russian soul (writing, miraculously, in Montenegrin) and describe her longing for Russian birch forests (the term coincides awkwardly with *Brezovik*, the name of a Montenegrin clinic for pulmonary diseases) and her own destiny.

My mischievous side would foist Derek Rubin's anthology on her, and I'd keep her on her toes by showering her with musings about the national and religious affiliation of writers; I'd bombard her with questions about what makes writing Jewish, Russian or Montenegrin, and whether literature can be compartmentalised in terms of cultural heritage – or is good writing inevitably secular and universal?

I'd make Zhenya think about whether a written text can have a Russian soul or a Jewish *neshama*. Whether humour and absurdity, which in the end never prevail over meaning, are traits of Jewish writing? What about Sartre and Camus, whose writings were not Jewish but by all means absurd? Does Russian literature stand out only by writing about guilt and turmoil? What are the features of Montenegrin writing? Can something that is characteristic of one of us be made the definition of us all? Will Montenegro ever produce easy writers, or are we doomed to big topics?

Contemporary Montenegrin literature is a relatively recent phenomenon – only in the nineties of the last century did our writers decide to remain in Montenegro, to live and write here (or perhaps circumstances forced them to do so).

Once it was not necessary to define Montenegrin identity; Montenegrins lived together with other Montenegrins, did business and married among themselves. But what does it mean to be a Montenegrin poet in the twenty-first century, when those limitations no longer exist?

Then there's the painful topic of assimilation. These are just some of the discourses that my Zhenya would deal with in her stories, which would certainly be good and honest, and Vova would accompany her and everything would be possible, even the end of the story, which they'd choose for themselves.

I release them here with all my love, whatever destiny they choose, and continue my life, which I live according to my own personal *siddur* or prayer book, in which the verses are my prayers and the stories my confessions – too spicy for the ears of priests and rabbis, and accessible only to readers; I continue to live by two calendars, in two worlds, with frequent pilgrimages to city bookshops to pay tribute to my saints: Pushkin, Nabokov and Aitmatov.

PS. Recently I received a letter from Uncle Vini, who now lives in Jerusalem. He's studying the Kabbalah and working on his memoirs. He took Zhenya's mother and grandmother with him because he didn't have the heart to leave them in Ignoransk. He sounds less grumblesome than before. Olya is an entrepreneur in the free world in partnership with Uncle Vini's runaway wife, while Lensky has published his third collection of poetry, which was well received by critics and, quite expectedly for our time, scooped a prestigious award and even made it onto the bestseller list.

'Zhenya' is a stand-alone section
from the 2016 novel *Šćer onoga bez đece*
(Daughter of the childless man)

Dana Todorović

REDUNDANCY

A strange device was delivered one morning to the dilapidated office of Jaroslav Smolarek, the secretary of a rural
municipality. It was a rectangular thing with a screen,
somewhat reminiscent of a modern television set, except
that this, although elegantly built, made the impression of
being a more primitive device due to its lack of a wheel
for adjusting the volume, nor did it have an antenna. It
is noteworthy, incidentally – though of little importance
for the overall story – that two other, quite independent
objects were delivered together with this device: a small
letterboard, which most officials agreed was an educational
aid for schoolchildren to learn the alphabet, and a rounded
thing whose purpose was difficult to ascertain; these two
items had obviously ended up in the wrong consignment,
so they were returned to the sender without delay via the
same courier.

In the letter from the head of the district, i.e. the sender,
Jaroslav Smolarek was instructed to replace the old typewriter with this device for the purpose of compiling weekly
reports on the activities of the municipality, and the letter
was accompanied by a Glossary to facilitate use of the new

device. Although at first glance the Glossary appeared to be an extremely incomprehensible text replete with abbreviations and convoluted borrowings from English, the board of the municipality had a nose for matters of importance, and bearing in mind that the only fact beyond any doubt was that it was impossible to type on this device, they quickly realised there was a deeper meaning hidden behind the order about the 'weekly report'. Therefore, in order to figure out the true meaning of the Glossary, the board convened an extraordinary meeting, and after an exhaustive discussion that lasted well into the night it drew the following conclusion, which consisted of three points. Firstly: the village would soon be ravaged by a terrible epidemic that could take the entire European continent back to the era of the plague, as evidenced by the myriad 'bugs', 'worms' and 'viruses' contained in the Glossary. Secondly: the mention of 'windows', 'firewalls' and other construction terms conveyed the message that it was necessary to build a shelter as protection against the impending pestilence. And thirdly: diplomatic terms such as 'resolution' and 'protocols' indicated unequivocally that they were dealing with a problem of global significance.

The truth about the weekly report flowed from this conclusion with glaring clarity, and at the end of the week the district head was delivered a report summing up the board's dedicated work on the secret task (neatly typed on an old typewriter – how else?). It listed 80 pairs of woollen socks, 20 litres of Dettol, 30 pairs of sterile gloves, 30 boxes of powdered milk and 120 candles. Two days later, the municipality received a directive stating that the whole business had been discontinued and that the device was to be returned to the district office, and some of the board members commented self-critically that they'd been so busy with drafting the report that they'd forgotten to fulfil their basic obligation, i.e. to build a shelter.

However, the device was never returned to the district office because an unusual set of circumstances early the next morning completely altered its fate. As the municipal office's caretaker, Bogumil Pliška, was passing by the device, he saw a warning flash on the screen: SYSTEM FAILURE. CHECK MOTHERBOARD. It should be elaborated that Bogumil was the scion of a noted apiarist family who was orphaned at the age of five when his parents were stung to death by a swarm of bees due to a faulty queen excluder – the grid that limits the movement of the hive's motherbee. All manner of repressed feelings had been piling up for years inside this unlucky janitor, who suffered from bizarre facial tics, and when he saw 'motherboard' flash in this ominous warning, it inevitably reminded him of the faulty grid and the mother of the beehive, causing him to relive the traumatic loss of his parents. He also simultaneously remembered the local hooligans tying him to a tree near the playground a few years later, him shitting his pants at a school event, and many other humiliations. All the pains of growing up suddenly came to the surface, and, not knowing how to ward off this rush of emotions, Bogumil instinctively grabbed a hammer from his toolkit and laid into the device with all his might.

At the waning of the day, the broken computer was dumped at the nearby landfill. The shards of the screen glistened in the ruddy light of the setting sun, leaving us to wonder: who (or what) emerged victorious from this short story?

Originally published in *NIN* magazine
on 23 May 2013

Jovanka Vukanović

EVERYTHING

Imagination is everything! How many times have we heard that? Mostly in literary soirées or playful programmes for children on TV. It's as if uttering this seemingly innocuous catchphrase lends the authors and presenters (and us together with them) greater authority in dealing with the life that tries and tests us by degrees every day. For me, the word 'everything' in the second part of this statement or truism, if we can call it that, has always been ambiguous and even triggered a certain unease in me, a restlessness, pangs in the bowels or uterus ... And you have to admit: 'anything' can be both beautiful and ugly, clever and stupid, harsh and gentle ... Just give free rein to your imagination and its combinations will leave you in awe! And that's just what happened on the garden terrace that day, when my husband and I, in silence, each in their own world, were thinking back on our days, which have long since started becoming more and more similar – it's hard to know which day is shabbier, pettier, more myopic or nervous than the next.

Two yards from the terrace was a storage shed, which we preferred to call a *little house*, whose doors were half-glazed, but its frame was badly weathered by the sun, wind and rain. It had been stabilised on several occasions with various kinds of tape: broad, pale-yellow masking tape, the sort that's half as wide, and the standard, grey Sellotape most often used for packaging, and there were also black, smooth, waterproof types of tape. But this colourful bouquet loosened over time – it adhered to the glass less and less, and each and every one of the strips sought release, a chance to fly and flitter away. Suddenly it seemed to me that it was no longer our little house but a sanctuary high up amidst the peaks of Nepal, Tibet or maybe the Andes (as I'd seen on TV – oh, that TV again), decorated with multicoloured prayer flags, tiles, bits of fabric …

The devil got hold of me – that's what I usually say when I get myself in a pickle – and I blurted:

'It's like we're in Nepal.'

'What do mean Nepal?'

'Because of all the fluttering ribbons.'

'Ah, that's you being ironical again.' (I saw he was starting to get it!)

'There's no irony, it's just a point of finding a tradesman to glaze it properly.'

'You're always fault-finding!'

'Not me. It's you who can't accept any comment …'

'That's enough of your whinging!'

'Let's be civil, shall we?'

'Hey? Oh, shove off and give me a breather!'

'So that's how far it's got!'

And it really had got that far.

The house with the colourful ribbons, the terrace, the garden, the fence – everything suddenly vaporised. Instead, salvoes of flaming insults engulfed everything in their path like a forest fire. All that remained was air, suffocating and hot, which we gulped greedily with our foaming mouths to try and overcome our harsh, hateful cries.

And *everything* came out. You can imagine ...

HOME
LIBRARIES

1.

His grandmother's concert piano takes centre stage in the house in Provence. The steps below are the fireplace, on the left is the dining room, and to the right is the dark-brown suite of furniture with the library. Among the books is an album. We browse though it together. We come across a photo of his mother lying naked on the bow of the ship. He says, cool and calm: 'That's Mother. She was beautiful when she was young.'

2.

He moved out from his parents', but he didn't take his books with him. I dropped by at his place after work and saw ten books on the table. New titles were supplied by his best friend, a poet, whose fine polo-neck jumpers and cognacs were financed by his mother. The first book was *Coños*. 'Pussies?' 'Uh-huh. I took it too. It's good. The first vignette is about a Gypsy woman's hot pussy. Wait, I'll read it to you.' My churning stomach and I listened to the story.

3.

'We lived near the Zetski Dom theatre. I'd glance at the roof next door. If it was wet I stayed home, if it was dry I went out to play. There were only Dostoyevsky and Tolstoy on the bookshelves – I didn't know about other cultures for a long time.'

4.

A fifteen-square-metre New York room for nine hundred dollars a month. Two tall, white shelves with books on photography. 'I don't have time to read them; I collect.'

5.

The bare glass shelves have been meticulously dusted. There is only a set of car keys in the corner of one, and the book *Danica* (Morning Star) at the beginning of the other. Danica is the name of their daughter.

6.

Her plates are black. The carpet is black. The shelves are black. The books are untouched. The curtains are heavy. The sink is clogged. Her high heels are worn out. The drawer is full of garish nail polishes.

7.

I take the Antwerp-Brussels train. When I arrive, I go by metro and finally reach the bookshop. The interior is playful but distracts from the books. I search for and find Stiglitz, Guillevic and Michaux, all in French. I hold them close to me and smell them. I pay at the counter and am given a thick, transparent bag. I can already imagine them in my library, in bed and on the floor. I take the metro back to the main station. I'll have coffee there, before returning to Antwerp, with a former colleague from the European Commission – an intellectual in a high position. I can't conceal my enthusiasm, and before we've even ordered I show him book after book. 'Thank you, what can I say,' he replies.

8.

I'd take one of Fromm's books from my grandfather's library. I don't know who to ask. Grandfather died. All of sudden, I hear silent Grandmother's voice.

9.

I moved from Paris with everything except one suitcase of books. I went back to collect it and lugged it on the metro to the Gare de Lyon. I told him I'd be coming back by train. We agreed to have coffee at the station. Whenever he met me, I had at least one suitcase with me, and that annoyed him. He felt he was a through station and didn't believe he was my most important entrance and exit. I got off the train. It was our first meeting in three years. The first thing he said was: 'You've changed your perfume.'

10.

She's become a little hunched and has extra girth; she's more quiet than talkative now; she involuntarily scratches the side of her thumb and hasn't painted her nails red in a long time; with people, she's tense and cautious; she prefers to sit and look out the window than explain the benefits of this and that credit card. Her friends and relatives raise their voices; they're angry and ask where her sense of self-worth is; they hold 'you-ought-to' speeches; they urge her to go to a pop concert; they criticise her because her private library is dusty. She wants them to hug her ... for more than a second. She wants to be told that her upper lip is beautiful when she smiles; she wants them to understand that sometimes she encounters burdens heavier than herself; she wants them to tell her that only she can notice that detail in the graffiti-filled lift; she wants them to take her out to that special terrace, never mind if she doesn't feel like wearing glasses; she wants them to trust that she knows best how to clean away the blackness in the cellar. But that won't happen. She's alone down there. Scrubbing. Clean concrete shows through.

11.

The house has been burgled several times. So far, the library hadn't been touched, but this time two leather-bound volumes of Njegoš's *The Mountain Wreath* disappeared. The old recipes from Budva are still there – who'd take a freezer bag full of yellowed cards? I open it and read, paying attention not to the procedures but to the language and measurements. 'Lemon zest', 'several sprigs of parsley', 'two bulblets of garlic', 'three gills of milk', 'a finger of oil'; 'mix together and plait a loaf'. I decided to make an Umberto cake. I love the feel of flour and the aroma of vanilla. I don't know if I bake more for the haptics or for comfort. It's ready. He won't even try it because he doesn't eat white sugar. She won't because she doesn't eat white flour. And they're not allowed to – they can't eat fat. The untouched crust goes hard.

Tijana Živaljević

12.

'She's a diplomat, so I appreciate she can't take her books from city to city every time she's sent on a mission. I've done her all over the flat. Otherwise, I can't screw a woman unless I see she's got a library.'

13.

'I know you've just moved in, but since you're a writer it's strange I don't see a single shelf with books.' 'I want to make real bookshelves, nicely sealed and behind glass, to preserve them. Not any old chipboard. Books deserve to be displayed and cared for properly. But right now I don't have the money – it's a costly business.' 'Where are they now?' 'In bags, down in the cellar.'

14.

I cleaned the dust off the soles. It made the suede too slippery. Now they were ready for the Student Cultural Centre dancefloor. I also packed a pair of those odd, baggy-tight pants. They're perfect for tango. They give you freedom in the hips and leave the feet clearly visible, ready for the quick movements of sacada. I arrived and went straight to the workshop hall. When it was over, I'd sleep at my godparents'. I was sure it would be over by one. We danced until seven in the morning. I put on my All-Stars. I carried a canvas bag with my high heels in one hand and my overnighter in the other. I felt every bump underfoot. The Belgraders were rushing to work. We head slowly to our godparents' or friends', to rented rooms or lovers' flats. I entered, and a neatly made double bed awaited me. My godparents were sleeping on the couch. I couldn't go to sleep, still quivering from the violin and the embraces. I thought of taking a book from their collection – it would calm me – but I couldn't see the books anywhere. I called my godmother on the phone: 'Where are all your books? I'd like to read something.' 'We hide them. They get stolen. You'll see a key in the ashtray. The closet is in the attic.'

15.

The shorter bathrobe stays with me. The longer one goes to him. I put the size thirty-nine slippers in the shoe cupboard. The forty-threes go to him. What should I do with the pictures? I don't know. The candlesticks stay with me. Everything of Miles Davis goes to him. The wine glasses – here. The Norwegian knife – there. The linen bags of lavender – into the wardrobe. The tie – into the suitcase. The globe – to me. The mannequin – to him. The flowers – onto the windowsill. The clay – into the suitcase. The library: Carver stays with me and Kotler goes to him. I sense the futility. The rubbish skip is nearby. I throw in a third batch. A Gypsy on a bicycle makes off with the globe.

16.

Like an archaeologist in an abandoned house, I pick up *Elena of Montenegro*. I see from the dedication that it was given as a gift, and then returned to Mother because it interested her most of all. Among the books on top of the wardrobe are a ceramic sculpture resembling the work of Claudel, a piece of old silver and brass picture frames. The wardrobe contains a fur coat, silk scarves from Lyon, a ball of white wool with the label 'Tetovo, Yugoslavia' and a broken radio. She didn't tell me the story of any of these objects; I could only sense the elegance in her appearance and movement, as well as her fear-shrouded silence. Mother died. I have to decide what to throw away and what to keep.

THE AUTHORS

Bojana Babić was born in 1990 in Pančevo (Serbia). She studied dramaturgy in Belgrade and wrote numerous filmscripts and plays that were staged there, including a dramatisation of *The Lord of the Flies*. Currently she lives in Canada and is pursuing a PhD in Screen Cultures and Curatorial Studies.

Marijana Čanak was born in 1982 in Subotica (Serbia) and studied literature in Novi Sad (Serbia). She works in adult education and writes prose. She has twice won the prestigious Laza K. Lazarević Prize for the best new short story in Serbia. Her main works to date are *Ulični prodavci ulica* (*Street vendors of Streets*, 2002), the short story collection *Pramatere* (*Matriarchs*, 2019) and the novel *Klara, Klarisa* (2022). She lives in Novi Sad and Novi Žednik.

Marijana Dolić was born in 1990 in Teslić (Bosnia-Herzegovina) and grew up in Sombor (Serbia). She writes poetry and prose fragments, lives in Belgrade and recently worked there at the KROKODIL Centre for Contemporary Literature. She considers life an eternal migration of peoples.

Zvonka Gazivoda, born in 1970 in Belgrade, has published numerous collections of short stories and poetry. Her 2020 debut novel *Hostel Kalifornija* (Hostel California) was shortlisted for the prestigious NIN Award, the European Union Prize for Literature and nominated for the regional Meša Selimović Prize. She lives in Belgrade.

Svetlana Kalezić-Radonjić was born in the Montenegrin capital, Podgorica, in 1980. She holds a PhD in Literature and is a professor at the University of Nikšić (Montenegro). She has written seven books of poetry, sings in a rock band, translates and enjoys travelling – 'in love with yesterday, today and tomorrow,' she writes. She lives in Podgorica.

Slađana Kavarić-Mandić was born in 1991 in Podgorica. She is currently completing her PhD on the philosophy of the Praxis School and creative Marxism. She writes short stories and poetry, and a first collection of her poems, *Ljudi niotkuda* ('People from Nowhere'), was published in 2016.

Olja Knežević is a Croatia-based Montenegrin novelist. Her 2019 novel *Katarina, velika i mala*, which received that year's V.B.Z. Award, was published by Istros Books the following year as *Catherine the Great and the Small*; it is considered the first contemporary novel by a Montenegrin woman author to be published in English translation. Her other novels include *Milena & Other Social Reforms* (2011) and *Mrs Black* (2015).

Jelena Lengold is a Serbian poet, novelist and journalist. A longtime cultural reporter for Radio Belgrade, Lengold has published a number of books, including poetry, novels and short stories. Her short story collection *Vašarski*

Mađioničar (Fairground Magician, Istros, 2015) won the EU Prize for Literature. She is also the author of two novels: *Baltimor* (Baltimore, 2003, 2011) and *Odustajanje* (Abandonment, 2018).

Ana Miloš was born in 1992 in Belgrade, where she also lives. She has written a collection of poetry, *Govori grad* ('The City Speaking', 2020) and a collection of short stories, *Kraj raspusta* ('The End of the Holidays', 2019, 2021), which was awarded the 2019 Đura Đukanov Prize for the best collection of short stories by a Serbian author aged under 30. Miloš's poems and stories have been published widely in magazines in the region.

Katarina Mitrović, born in 1991 in Belgrade, is a screenwriter and playwright. She studied Serbian language and literature and is currently completing a degree in drama. She has published two books of poetry, *Utroba* (Womb, 2017) and *Dok čekam da prođe* (While I wait for this to pass, 2018). Her experimental novel in verse, *Nemaju sve kuće dvorište* (Not all houses have a courtyard, 2020) was well received. She co-authored the script for the upcoming mystery-thriller *Deca zla* (Children of evil). She lives in Belgrade.

Andrea Popov-Miletić was born in 1985 in Novi Sad (Serbia), where she also lives. She studied literature and was a student journalist; now she writes short stories, novels, diaries and stories for children that are broadcast on Radio Belgrade. Her 2019 novel *Pioniri maleni, mi smo morska trava* ('Young Pioneers, We are Seaweed') was longlisted for the NIN Award and shortlisted for the national Zlatni suncokret (Golden Sunflower) Prize.

Milica Rašić, born in 1989, lives and works in Niš (Serbia). After studying philosophy, she works as an auxiliary school teacher and a translator from English and French.

Svetlana Slapšak is a Belgrade-born writer, translator, editor, anthropologist and activist, now based in Slovenia. She has written over 70 books, including the popular mock-adventure novel *Leon i Leonina* (Leon and Leonine), novels and academic works in the field of anthropology. In 1993, Slapšak was named a recipient of the PEN/Barbara Goldsmith Freedom to Write Award.

Lena Ruth Stefanović was born in 1970 in Belgrade. She studied Russian literature and diplomacy in Belgrade, Sofia and Moscow. She lives in Podgorica, works as a translator/interpreter, and is a productive poet and prose writer – as well as a cultural activist. Her latest novel, *Aimée*, was published in 2020.

Dana Todorović is a half-Serbian, half-American novelist living in Belgrade. Her debut novel *Tragična sudbina Morica Tota* ('The Tragic Fate of Moritz Toth', Istros 2016) was shortlisted for the Branko Ćopić Prize for best novel, awarded annually by the Serbian Academy of Sciences and Arts, and was also listed as one of the top novels of the year by the NIN weekly and the daily *Politika*. Her second novel, *Park Logovskoj*, was shortlisted for major literary awards, including the NIN.

Jovanka Vukanović was born near Knin, in what is now Croatia. She studied French and Yugoslav literature at the University of Zadar. To date she has published five collections of poetry, as well as two books of essays and reviews.

A third book of her essays and criticism, *Od riječi do knjige* ('From Word to Book'), is soon to be published. She lives in Podgorica.

Tijana Živaljević was born in 1985 in the historical Montenegrin capital of Cetinje, where she also lives. She is a macro-economist by training and has travelled widely. She works as a translator, interpreter and tourist guide. Živaljević is an avid writer when she finds the time, and her prose work *Dijalozi u Crnoj Gori* (self-translated as 'Dialogues about Montenegro') deserves mention.

THE TRANSLATOR

Will Firth was born in Newcastle, Australia, in 1965. He focuses on contemporary writing from the Serbo-Croatian speaking countries and North Macedonia. He graduated in German, Russian and Serbo-Croatian from the Australian National University in Canberra. He won a scholarship to read South Slavic studies at the University of Zagreb in 1988-89 and spent a further postgraduate year at the Pushkin Institute in Moscow in 1989-90. Since 1990 he has been living in Germany, where he works as a freelance translator of literature and the humanities. He translates from Russian, Macedonian and all variants of Serbo-Croatian. In 2005-07 he worked for the International Criminal Tribunal for the former Yugoslavia. Firth is a member of professional associations of translators in Germany (VdÜ) and the UK (Translators Association). His best-received translations of recent years have been Aleksandar Gatalica's *The Great War*, Faruk Šehić's *Quiet Flows the Una* and Tatjana Gromača's *Divine Child*.   www.willfirth.de